A K
CHRISTMAS

Featuring The Winter Wish
and The Risqué Resolution

JILLIAN EATON

© 2017 by Jillian Eaton
www.jillianeaton.com

ISBN: 9781973217480

Printed in the U.S.A.

May the holidays bring you warmth
and cheer that fills your
heart for the coming
New Year.

THE
WINTER
WISH

A Regency Holiday Novella

JILLIAN EATON

CHAPTER ONE

"SARAH, YOU ARE DOING IT AGAIN."

Glancing sideways at her best friend, Sarah made a face and sighed. "I know," she admitted, twisting her hands anxiously on her lap. "But I simply cannot help it. He is so very *handsome*, Lily. Do you not think he is handsome?" With another little sigh, this one dreamier than the last, Sarah returned to staring unabashedly at Lord Devlin Heathcliff as he waltzed across the ballroom floor.

Strikingly tall with a well-muscled physique to match, the Viscount of Winswood had been blessed with glossy brown hair, piercing blue eyes, and two matching dimples. His jawline was strong, his nose straight. From the top of his head to the tips of his boots he was sheer perfection in every way, shape, and form. It was a fact he knew very well and used to his full advantage at every opportunity, especially where women were concerned.

As Sarah watched, her face all but green with envy, the slender brunette in his arms threw back her head and tittered. The Viscount drew her close to whisper something in her ear and she laughed again, this time loudly enough to cause a few heads to swivel. Fearing she could be caught gaping Sarah turned in the uncomfortable wooden chair she had been sitting on since the ball began some hours before and exchanged a rueful smile with Lily.

"I think Lady Roland has big ears and an absolutely vile temper," her friend said loyally, referring to the brunette upon whose neck Devlin's lips were currently resting. "Not to worry, Sarah. She will be nothing more than yet another passing fancy. You know how he is with them, like a child with a shiny new toy. At the last ball it was Lady Awning, remember? And before that Lady Newmore caught his eye for all of five minutes." Leaning forward, Lily took Sarah's hand and squeezed it tight. "You will have your chance, not to worry. Although—" her dark eyebrows lifted knowingly "—your chance would come a lot more quickly if you ever actually got up the nerve to *speak* to him."

Every fiber of Sarah's body rebelled at the idea of talking to the man who she had been in love with since her sixteenth birthday when she first saw him from across a crowded room. That had been seven years ago when she was a young debutante with stars in her eyes and hope in her heart. Now those stars were long since extinguished, and the hope… Her shoulders slumped. The hope was all but gone as well.

"You know I could never do that," she said in a whisper, lest the other unfortunate wallflowers who hovered around them overhear. Fretting with a long blond curl that had come undone from her coiffure, she peeked sideways at Devlin one more time before looking away with a little gasp. Had *he* been staring at *her*? Surely not. The very idea was inconceivable. Impossible, even. And yet…

Holding her breath, she dared one more glance. For an instant her heart slammed against her ribcage as she saw he truly *was* facing her, but his gaze… Oh, drats. His gaze was focused on Lily.

"He is looking at you," she said glumly.

"Who is?"

"Lord Heathcliff."

Her friend snorted in unladylike disbelief. "He is not. He is merely – oh, well I never. *Sarah*," she hissed, her violet eyes widening with ill-disguised excitement, "he is walking over here, right now! What do you want me to do?"

It was of no surprise to any of the wallflowers, least of all Sarah, that amidst all of the women who spent every ball sequestered away in a corner of the room it was Lily who would manage to attract attention of the masculine variety. After all, she was not *truly* a wallflower. No, she was much too pretty to be one of them with her long flowing black hair, heart shaped face, and eyes the color of amethysts. She sat with them out of loyalty, and because she and Sarah had been the best of friends since childhood.

"Dance with him," Sarah said, giving Lily a little push. "Quickly, before he changes his mind and goes somewhere else."

In a flurry of yellow skirts Lily rose to her feet, but she paused to look back at Sarah, a troubled frown pulling her tipping the corners of her mouth down. "Are you certain? I would never want to—"

"Go," Sarah said firmly. "If I cannot dance with him, the next best thing is having you do it for me."

Lily's entire face lit up. "I will return as soon as it is over to tell you all about it," she vowed.

"I want to hear every single detail, so do not forget

anything. Now go!" As Sarah watched Lily flounce away, she could not help but smile, and her happiness was truly genuine. She wished only good things for her friend, and what could be better than spending even a moment in Devlin's arms?

He approached Lily with a panther like grace, his long legged gait more a prowl than a saunter, and Sarah nearly tipped out of her chair as she strained forward in vain to hear what words were being exchanged as he murmured something to Lily and she smiled in reply.

Then they were dancing, and when Devlin curved his arm around the slim hollow of Lily's back Sarah felt as though he were holding *her*. And when Lily laughed at something amusing he whispered in her ear Sarah felt as though *she* were laughing too. It was as wonderful as it was gut wrenchingly horrible, for in that moment Sarah was forced to acknowledge that this was the closest she would ever come to being wrapped in the arms of the man she so desperately – and foolishly – loved.

When the waltz ended Devlin bowed and Lily curtsied. They parted ways, and Sarah waited in white knuckled anticipation to hear everything. Unable to sit still, she met Lily halfway across the ballroom floor, sucking in her belly to squeeze between dancers and ducking low under silver trays heavy with refreshments.

"Not here," she said when she finally reached Lily and her friend's mouth opened. "Come with me." Hand in hand the two women darted out a side door and, laughing like children, ran down the long, candlelit hallway until they reached an empty room.

Like the rest of the Harcourt Estate upon which the ball was being held, the study they had stumbled upon was immaculately decorated with gilded framed paintings, matching love seats in deep burgundy, and an impressive mahogany desk that boasted neatly piled stacks of parchment and a half dozen leather bound books.

Flames smoldered in the floor to ceiling fireplace and Sarah jolted the embers awake with a poker while Lily launched into a lively retelling of every second that had transpired between her and the Viscount.

"...and then," she said, rather breathless from the excitement of it all, "he touched my hand. Well, all of my fingers, except for the thumb. And he said..."

"Yes?" Sarah gave the fire an extra hard poke. "What did he say?"

"He said '*You are a lovely dancer*'. Can you believe it?"

"You *are* a lovely dancer," Sarah pointed out reasonably.

"But to hear it from him, it truly meant—oh dear, I am sorry." Her lower lip jutting out, Lily crossed the room in three quick strides and looped her arm around Sarah's shoulders, which were undeniably slumped. "It should have been you," she murmured softly. "It should have been you, and here I have been blathering on about it like a shrew. Forgive me, dearest."

Sarah shrugged. "I wanted to know."

Turning to face the fire, both women held out their hands to warm them as they fell into reflective silence. Outside the windows the wind howled, a reminder that beyond the toasty confines of the study winter was unleashing her wrath. It was the second week of December, and the Season had just begun.

For Sarah it would be her seventh, for Lily her fifth. A decade of failed Seasons between them, and this one was not looking any more promising than the last. It did not help that Sarah possessed all the temerity of a field mouse and Lily, while much more confident around men, refused to accept the attentions of anyone unless Sarah was being courted as well. Since that had yet to happen, they were both very much 'on the shelf' which was not a place any woman under the age of thirty desired to be.

"I wish…" Sarah began, but she stopped herself short, unable to give voice to the secret desire that burned within her.

"You wish what?" Lily prompted.

Sarah nibbled on her bottom lip before she said, "I wish Devlin would simply notice me. I wish he would look up and see me, as he sees those other women. As he saw you. As I see him." Sighing, she shook her head. "I know it is folly, but there it is."

Drawing back her shoulders so she stood at her full height of five feet, three inches Lily pinned her hands to her hips and drew her eyebrows together over the bridge of her nose. "I think that is a fine wish, Sarah Emily Dawson, and you should not think otherwise, do you hear me?"

"Perhaps," Sarah allowed softly. "But it will never come true."

"You never know," Lily said, smiling mysteriously. "'Tis the season for miracles… And I think we are both due for a little magic."

CHAPTER TWO

THE NEXT AFTERNOON Lily called on Sarah for tea, and after sating their hunger with crumpets drizzled in honey the two women dressed in their warmest cloaks, complete with fur lined hoods and cozy matching muffs, to brave the winter chill.

It had snowed overnight and everything, from the dormers on the rooftops to the lamp posts that guarded every street corner, was blanketed in a soft, pristine white. Carriages pulled by prancing horses flew past, while children armed with snowballs waged war and a group of carolers made their way from house to house, singing merrily of silver bells and Old Saint Nicholas. Lily's spinster aunt attended them as chaperone, but the poor dear was so deaf it was rather like having no one watch them at all. She stayed behind them, her nose more often than not buried in a book, and every once in a while Lily would have to turn and trot back to guide her aunt back onto the correct path.

"I love this time of year," Lily sighed as she neatly sidestepped a pile of discarded soot. "It is so filled with hope and promise. Why, it feels as though anything is possible!"

Sarah, who tended to be much more practical minded than her friend, tried not to scowl. Her toes were freezing and she was fairly certain her nose was about to fall right off her face despite the three separate scarves she had wrapped around her neck.

For her, Christmastime invoked a very different response than it did for Lily. While everyone else was coming together, she had never felt more alone. Seeing men and women arm in arm, their faces flushed from the cold and their eyes sparkling with love, she was reminded of what she did not have: namely, Devlin Heathcliff. And even though it was silly and ridiculous and she knew nothing would ever come of it, she could not help but wonder what he was doing this very minute.

No doubt he was wrapped in the arms of his lover. They would be in front of a fireplace, Sarah decided. Quite naked, of course, with only each other's bodies and a shared glass of wine to warm them. It was a decadent scene for someone with her limited experience to imagine, but imagine it she did: once, twice, three times a

16

day at the very least.

What would it feel like to have Devlin's lips press against her throat? To have his hands sweep down her body, lingering on the curve of her collarbone before slowly going lower to cup her breasts and then lower still, to—

"Sarah, you are blushing," Lily observed with great interest. "Why are you blushing?"

"I… I feel quite flushed," Sarah lied. Oh dear. How dreadfully embarrassing.

"You do? Splendid!" Sliding her hands out of her fur muff and tucking it under one arm, Lily reached up to secure her hood more tightly around her dark curls. "I was afraid you were getting cold – you know how sensitive you can be – but if you are feeling warm, we can continue on to the park. I even brought a few crumpets along to feed the geese." Reaching into the pocket of her cloak she procured three pastries and held one out to Sarah, who took it with a smile that felt more like a grimace, but if Lily noticed she made no sign. "Aunt Ingrid," she called over her shoulder, "we are going to the park."

The woman trailing behind them temporarily lowered the book she was holding pressed to her nose and bobbed her head with a vague smile.

"Cannot hear a word, poor dear," Lily said. "But she'll follow along.

Like the rest of London the park was covered in white although there were fewer people here than on the streets. Small songbirds, their brightly colored fluff standing out in sharp contrast against the plain backdrop, hopped from tree to tree, twittering a merry song as they flitted about. Spying a bright red cardinal amidst the skeletal branches Sarah pointed it out to Lily, who smiled and threw a piece of crumpet.

They had nearly reached the lake when, without warning, a narrow sleigh pulled by a wild eyed horse went flying past, so close that snow spewed out from beneath the blades, showering Sarah and Lily in a thick gray slush.

"Why I never!" Lily cried, staring down at her ruined cloak in dismay.

Of equal sentiment, Sarah threw back her hood and gasped as she felt a slow, slippery trickle of wet snow slide down her spine. The *nerve* of some people! Why, if she ever met the driver of the sleigh she would give him a piece of her—

"Look, he is turning around. Sarah, take this." Holding

out her hand warmer, Lily gathered up her skirts and began to walk determinedly towards the horse and sleigh which had come to a halt less than ten yards away.

Her eyes wide and her heart pounding, Sarah scurried after her friend, all thoughts of speaking her mind completely erased now that the opportunity had actually presented itself. She stopped short beside Lily, anxiously twisting the muff back and forth in her hands as they waited for the driver to dismount.

He did so slowly, swinging one leg out the open door of the sleigh and then the other before easing down to the ground. Securing the reins, he removed his hat, unwound a green scarf from his neck, and pivoted to face them, an apologetic smile already laying claim to his sensual lips. "Ladies, I do apologize," he said smoothly, lifting one dark eyebrow. "Forgive me?"

Sarah felt her knees wobble. Thankfully Lily was right beside her and without missing a beat the brunette reached out to steady her friend. "Remain calm," she hissed out of the corner of her mouth. "And for heavens sakes whatever you do, do *not* faint. Lord Heathcliff," she said loudly. "What an unexpected… surprise."

Devlin took a step closer to them, his smile growing distantly polite as his piercing blue eyes gave a cursory sweep of Sarah before focusing solely on Lily. "Have I had the pleasure of making your acquaintance? Surely not," he continued, answering his own question before Lily could get a word in edgewise, "for how could I forget such a beautiful face as yours?"

It did not escape either woman that Devlin spoke directly to Lily, ignoring Sarah as if she had simply ceased to exist (which was just fine with Sarah as she feared she was currently incapable of speaking a word) but Lily was not about to overlook the Viscount's poor manners so easily.

Lifting her chin, the violet eyed beauty said scathingly, "You danced with me this evening past, Lord Heathcliff. Had I realized you possessed such a forgetful memory, I would have no doubt chosen a different partner."

Visibly caught off guard, Devlin blinked once, twice, and cleared his throat. "I, uh, well then. Yes, yes now I remember. Lady… Dresher, if I am not mistaken?"

"Kincaid," Sarah squeaked out unexpectedly. "Her name is Lady Kincaid."

Immediately she felt two sets of eyes upon her, and her cheeks burned a bright red in response. Oh no. She had done it. She had actually spoken to Devlin. No, not simply spoken to him... Corrected him! Oh, this was all wrong. All terribly, terribly wrong. "I mean," she gasped, staring blindly at a spot in the snow a good foot to the right of where Devlin was standing, "her n-name could e-easily be mistaken for Lady Dresher as they do sound quite s-similar."

"They do not sound at all alike," the viscount said dryly, taking both women by surprise, "and it was impossibly rude of me not to remember. Please, Lady Kincaid. Accept my sincerest apology."

Beside her, Sarah felt Lily relax. "Oh, very well. I suppose it must be difficult placing names with the faces of all the women you have danced with. Although," she said, holding up one finger, "I shall accept your apology on only one condition."

"Which is?" Devlin asked.

"You take my dearest friend for a ride in your sleigh."

Sarah felt her knees buckle. Of all the outlandish, inappropriate, ridiculous—

"Certainly," Devlin agreed. "If," he continued, flashing a dimple as he smiled while Sarah tried desperately not to swoon, "you accompany us as well."

"I am frightened of horses," Lily said, blinking innocently. "But Sarah just adores them, do you not

Sarah?"

It was a lie. It was *Lily* who loved horses, not Sarah. Sarah was terrified of them ever since she had taken a particularly nasty spill from a stubborn mare some years before. She opened her mouth to say exactly that and received a quick jab in the side courtesy of Lily's elbow. "I... I love horses," she said weakly. "They... They are m-marvelous creatures."

Devlin look at her a little oddly, but Lily beamed. "There, you see? They are, after all, her favorite animal and she is quite the accomplished equestrian. Why, I have never seen a better rider."

A glimmer of interest surfaced in Devlin's eyes. For the first time he looked at Sarah directly and the full force of that piercing gaze was enough to have her swaying on her feet. "Do you hunt?" he asked.

"Do I w-what?"

"Hunt," he repeated. "On horseback. Do you hunt?"

"Oh, she goes hunting all the time," Lily interceded, giving Sarah's arm a tight squeeze through her cloak. "It is her favorite thing to do. Right, dearest?"

Sarah blinked. What was Lily saying? She could not focus when Devlin was looking at her as if she were the only woman within a hundred miles. He grinned, showing both dimples this time, and she stopped breathing. "Yes," she said dazedly. "It is my most favorite thing."

"Excellent," the viscount declared. "I have never met a woman who enjoyed that particular activity before. Perhaps you can tell me about your last outing while I take you around the park. When should I call on you?"

Sarah opened her mouth to reply, but Lily beat her to it. "Why waste time?" she chirped, waving a hand in the air. "The weather can be so finicky. Go now, while there is enough snow on the ground. Go," she repeated, giving Sarah a little push forward, "and have a wonderful time. You can bring her to Twinings when you are finished."

Twinings, a small tea shop on the outskirts of the park, was a favorite winter destination for those seeking a temporary respite from the cold.

"Lily I cannot," Sarah hissed, looking desperately back over her shoulder. The very idea of being in the close confines of the sleigh alone with Devlin thrilled her even as it terrified her. Never in her wildest dreams had she ever imagined speaking to him, let alone being near enough to touch! What would she do? What would she *say*? It was too daunting a task to even comprehend. Not knowing what to do or where to turn she remained frozen in place, her gaze flicking helplessly from Devlin to Lily and back again.

"You are such a dear for remembering to return my muff," Lily said loudly. Grabbing Sarah's hand she pulled her in close under the guise of having her hand warmer returned. "Now you listen to me," she whispered fiercely. "This is your chance, Sarah! *This* is your wish come true."

Sarah blanched. "I do not think—"

"When will an opportunity like this ever arise again? You and Lord Heathcliff." Her eyes fairly gleamed. "Alone in a sleigh with nothing but a shared blanket to keep you warm. Now go on, before I remember I have a great affinity for horses and love to fox hunt."

"Are you coming or not?" Devlin queried. He had returned to see to his horse and was scratching the large gray on the side of the neck. "Lady Kincaid, if you have changed your mind and would like to accompany us…" he ventured in an undeniably hopeful tone.

"No, no." Lily spun to face him, muff in hand, and smiled brilliantly. "I see some of my friend's right over there," she claimed, pointing to the left where a trio of heavily cloaked women and one man were walking. "I will see you at Twinings! Come along, Aunt Ingrid." And she was off without so much as a backwards glance, leaving Sarah completely and utterly alone.

She watched, incapable of saying a word, as Devlin moved to the side of the sleigh and held open the door. When he looked up at her expectantly she swallowed hard and walked jerkily towards him, feeling as though her limbs were being controlled by strings.

"Thank you," she managed to croak when he helped her up onto the small leather bench seat and laid a thick fur blanket across her lap.

"Will that keep you warm enough?" he asked, glancing sideways at her after he had climbed in from the opposite side and gathered up the reins.

Sarah managed a slight nod. "Yes, this will do quite n-nicely."

"Hold on tight," Devlin suggested, and with a snap of the whip they were off.

CHAPTER THREE

OF ALL THE different scenarios Sarah had imagined in her head when she dreamed of meeting Devlin, racing in an open sleigh had never been one of them.

Now she knew why.

Despite Lily's prediction to the contrary, there was nothing romantic about huddling under a fur blanket while slowly freezing to death. Within moments she could no longer feel her toes or her fingers, and her teeth were chattering so badly she feared she would bite her tongue in half.

Sarah supposed the scenery would have been nice to look at, except they were moving so fast that the snow covered pine trees and rolling hills had been reduced to little more than a mixed blur of green and white. It was making her quite dizzy, if she were to be perfectly honest, and after the second lap around the park she simply shut her eyes and prayed for it all to be over.

"You can look now. We have stopped." There was a

husky note of laughter in Devlin's voice, and when Sarah tentatively opened her eyes she saw he was grinning at her, his blue eyes filled with amusement. "You do not like horses, do you?" he asked, and in the face of such a blunt question without Lily to lie for her, Sarah was forced to shake her head.

"No," she admitted softly, looking down at her lap. "I am rather afraid of them."

They had stopped in the middle of a small clearing. The snow around them was untouched, indicating they were the first to venture to this particular spot since it had snowed the night before. In the distance Sarah could hear the raised voices of children and guessed they were somewhere close to the small skating pond where she had taken many a tumble as a little girl with skates that were too big and hand-me-down skirts that were too long.

She peeked at Devlin, hoping he would not be angry with her for fibbing. The Viscount certainly did not *appear* angry. If anything he looked more handsome than ever with his cheeks flushed red from the cold and his hair blown back by the wind. Without warning he turned his head to the side and caught her studying him. Their gazes held for one breathless moment, before Devlin smiled slowly and nodded down to the fur blanket Sarah had wrapped tightly around her legs.

"Do you mind?" he asked.

"N-no."

She felt his knee bump against her knee as he unfolded the blanket followed by the hard length of his thigh pressing against her thigh. Despite the cold air she could feel her face burning and she feigned interest in a tall pine tree so she had an excuse to turn her face aside, not wanting Devlin to see the effect his nearness had on her body. She heard him sigh, long and low, before he clucked to the horse and they started moving once again, this time at a much more leisurely pace.

"Why would you choose to go for a sleigh ride if you do not like horses?" he asked.

Beside him Sarah stiffened and began to anxiously thread her fingers through the long hairs on the blanket as she thought desperately of what Lily would say. "I... I... That is, you... Well, I do not quite..."

"I take it you do not fox hunt either," he said, turning to face her and raising one brow.

Feeling utterly miserable, Sarah shook her head.

"You are quite honest when you are not in the company of Lady Kincaid," he observed with a grin, and despite her nervousness Sarah found herself offering the shyest of smiles. "And you look quite pretty when you do that," he added, his gaze dropping to her lips. His expression turned quizzical, as if his own words had caught him by surprise, before he shrugged and urged his horse into a trot with a cluck of his tongue.

Silently cursing the blush that refused to leave her cheeks, Sarah ducked her head and looked out over the edge of the sleigh. Twenty-three years of age, she thought with a frustrated groan, and she still acted like a brand new debutante complete with a red face and the most ridiculous of stammers.

It was little wonder Devlin had never so much as looked at her before now, and she had little doubt that once they reached Twinings he would ever have reason to speak to her again. *Hopeless*, she told herself. *You are absolutely hopeless.*

"I do not even know your name," Devlin said suddenly, raising his voice to be heard above the sliding of the sleigh's rails against the snow and the merry jingle of the horse's harness. They had completed their circle of the park and were drawing closer to Twinings with every prancing step.

"Does it matter?" she muttered.

A frown turned his mouth down at the corners. "What

was that?"

Taking a deep breath, Sarah twisted in the seat to face him. If this was to be the last time they were in each other's company – which she was quite certain it would be – then it was high time she grew some steel in her spine and stopped behaving like a cowardly child. "I asked does it matter? My name," she clarified when he continued to look bemused. "You have already proven you do not have a great affinity for remembering a woman's name. Why then should I bother to waste my time telling you mine? You shall forget it the moment I step foot from the sleigh, or perhaps even before then." Her shoulders lifted and fell beneath her cloak in a small shrug. "Who is to say?"

Oh, she had done it now! What had gotten *into* her? Immediately Sarah felt contrite for being so uncharacteristically rude, and she half expected Devlin to bring the sleigh to a screeching halt and demand she walk to the tea shop. When he said nothing she drew her bottom lip between her teeth, worrying it back and forth until she could not take the silence any longer. "I do apologize. I do not know what came over—"

"Stop," Devlin demanded, switching the reins over to his left hand so he could raise his right, the palm facing

30

towards her. His fingers were long and lean, the tips of them calloused. Absently Sarah wondered what he did to have the hands of a common laborer, for it was well known amidst the *Ton* that he had no reason to work. His wealth was old and quite well established, more so now than ever before since his father had passed and he inherited the late Viscount's title. It was little wonder that women were constantly throwing themselves at him, although as far as Sarah was concerned he could have been a pauper.

Money mattered little to her and while she considered herself quite fortunate to be born into the upper class she did not allow her breeding to define her as so many other members of the peerage did. Were Devlin a duke or a farmer she was confident her feelings for him would remain unchanged… not that it mattered much now.

"Stop doing what?" she asked in confusion. "Stop apologizing?" Her gaze fell to her lap. "I truly am sorry, I usually never—"

"No. Stop doing that… with your lip," he said, gesturing vaguely. "It is quite… distracting." He scowled, as if he did not *want* to find it distracting, and was annoyed that he did.

She blinked. "I did not realize I was doing anything—

"

"There! There, you are doing it again."

Flustered by the sudden anger in his voice, Sarah covered her mouth with her hand as though by doing so she could keep the wrong words in and let only the right ones out. Speaking between her fingers she said, "I think it would be best if you brought me to Twinings now."

Devlin's jaw clenched. "I think that would be best as well," he agreed tersely. Taking the reins in both hands he slapped them against the gray's rump. The horse arched its neck and sprang into a trot with such force that Sarah flew back in the seat and her arms flew out, one striking the door of the sleigh rather painfully while the other landed in Devlin's lap.

"Oh," she gasped, frozen in shock as she saw the very intimate place her hand was now resting. "I... I did not mean... I am *so* sorry I... I..." Her voice trailed away as Devlin once again transferred the reins to his left hand and used the right to close his fingers around her wrist.

"Your pulse is pounding," he observed, tracing the pad of his thumb under the edge of her glove and down across the delicate veins on the inside of her wrist. "And you cannot stop stuttering. Do I make you nervous?"

"Nervous?" Sarah repeated. Their eyes caught, plain

brown against deep pools of blue, and she swallowed convulsively. "N-n-no."

"Liar," he whispered.

As Sarah watched, feeling as though she were in some sort of trance, Devlin lifted her hand and pressed his lips ever so slightly to her chilled skin. "You taste of apricots," he murmured, "and sunshine on a cold winter's day."

"*Oh*," Sarah breathed, unable to think of a single thing to say. Her lips parted on a sigh, and as suddenly as he had taken her hand, Devlin released it. He straightened and the length of his body went rigid while all emotion slipped from his face as though it were carved from stone.

"Trot on now," he said to the gray, while to Sarah he spoke not a word, nor spared a single glance, and they rode the rest of the way to Twinings in silence.

CHAPTER FOUR

TRY AS HE MIGHT, Devlin could not stop thinking about the shy, doe eyed girl he had met three days past. He did not know why she invaded his every waking moment, nor how she could be present in every dream. After all, there was nothing memorable about her. Her features were unremarkable at best, plain at worst. She had barely spoken more than ten words during the time they spent together and unlike the other women he tended to keep company with she was not flirtatious or provocative. *Then why*, he thought, crumpling a piece of parchment in his fist upon where he had been struggling to pen a letter for the past hour, *can I not forget her?*

And he did not even know her name.

He *did* know she smelled more sweetly than anything he had ever come across, and when he slept his dreams were consumed by fields of sunflowers and sunshine and her, laughing with her hair unbound in a tangle of gold as she ran towards him.

"Bloody hell," he growled. Standing, he began to pace across the length of his study, his hands clenched in fists at his side and his spine ramrod straight. He knew why he was so unsettled, though he dare not admit it aloud. He dared not speak *her* name aloud. So he said it in his mind... *Moira...* and it was a curse more than a name, which was fitting.

Moira, the first woman he had ever loved.

Moira, the first woman to own him body and soul.

Moira, the first woman to rip his heart from his chest while it was still beating and cast it aside on the ground as if it were no more than a common piece of refuse.

Eight years had passed since he got down on bended knee and asked that she-devil to marry him. Eight years since she laughed in his face and knocked the very ring from his hand. He could still remember what she had said as if it were yesterday, and even though he closed his eyes and willed the words away, he could not escape them.

"Marry you, a common viscount? I am the daughter of a duke, you fool. Would you have me marry a farmer? Or a gardener? For it would surely be the same thing. I never knew you were so stupid, Devlin."

"But Moira I... I love you. I want to be with you.

35

Spend my life with you."

"And you can, darling. In my bed. Now get up, you are embarrassing yourself."

Devlin's jaw hardened as he cast the ugly memory aside. Moira had been a greedy bitch, and he a besotted fool. When she became engaged to the Marquess of Bainsborough a week later he vowed never to put himself at a woman's mercy again. He had yet to break that promise.

Oh, he still liked women well enough, both behind closed doors and out. They were frivolous, fanciful creatures meant to be enjoyed and never taken seriously. It was why he made it a point never to remember their names, or show preference to one over the rest. The moment the dance was over or they left his bed he forgot about them as one might forget what they had for dinner the night before. It had been that way for eight long years… Until three days ago.

"Reynolds, get in here," he called as he forced his fists to unclench and his body to relax. Within moments there was a faint knock at the door. "Come in."

Reynolds – the faithful butler of the Heathcliff family for more than three generations – stepped into the room and came to attention. Short and heavy set, with the jowls of a bulldog and all the bite of a poodle, the servant looked his young employer up and down with the same quick, careful appraisal he had been giving Devlin since he was no more than a squalling babe.

"Something wrong, my lord?" he asked observably, for even though the viscount could appear at ease to the casual observer, Reynolds knew what simmered beneath the surface.

Devlin had the same temper of his father, and his father before him. All intelligent, successful, and kind men who treated their staff with respect and strove for fairness in everything they did. But they were also men who guarded their true feelings and, although slow to anger, were quite unforgiving when provoked.

Crossing his arms, Devlin leaned against the edge of his desk and cocked one eyebrow. "Nothing ever gets past you, does it Reynolds?"

"Very rarely," the butler acknowledged solemnly.

Devlin's lips twitched, but he did not smile. "I need someone found."

"Someone, my lord?"

"A female someone. A young woman," Devlin clarified. "In her mid-twenties, if I had to guess. I do not know her name, but her friend is Lady Connor. No, that is wrong. Not Connor… But something similar…" Damn it. What had been the chit's name? He should have remembered it instantly. After all, she had been the prettier of the two. But whenever he tried to think of her the only thing that came to mind was a pair of shy brown eyes and a Cupid's bow mouth. "Kinsman… Kinswood… Kin… Kin… Kincaid!" he said triumphantly as the name came to him at last. "Lady Kincaid. Do you know who she is?"

Reynolds' lips pressed together beneath his moustache. "Should I, my lord?"

"No, I suppose not." Devlin frowned. "Although it would make this much easier if you did. There is a ball tonight at Almack's, is there not Reynolds?"

The butler nodded.

"Lady Kincaid should be there. She was at the last one. Was I planning on attending?"

"I do not believe so."

"Well, now I am."

If Reynolds was surprised by this sudden change of events, it did not show in his face. "I will make the necessary arrangements, my lord. Your carriage will be brought round in one hour."

"One hour?" Devlin repeated. "Bloody hell, what time

is it?"

"Half past nine."

"Half past nine… You do not say. I had best get dressed then."

"Indeed."

Leaning across the desk to pick up his jacket which he had flung carelessly across the back of a chair, Devlin tucked it under one arm. He paused at the door. "Oh, and Reynolds, one last thing."

Reynolds waited, salt and pepper eyebrows raised expectantly.

"Stop 'my lording' me all the time. It is damn annoying of you."

Wisely, the butler waited until Devlin had exited the room to say, "As you wish, my lord."

"I DO NOT KNOW," Sarah said doubtfully as she swiveled in front of the full length mirror to peer at her back. "I feel terribly… exposed."

"Nonsense." Clapping her hands together, Lily studied her friend's reflection with a critical eye. What she saw made her grin. For once in her life, she had been able to talk Sarah into showing off her curvaceous figure. The ball gown, dark purple as a plum and fitted like a glove, was the perfect match for Sarah's blond hair and ivory complexion.

"Who knew you had such large... ears?" Lily continued, smiling mischievously when Sarah gasped in dismay and clutched her earlobes.

"Do you think so?"

"Darling, I was not talking about your ears." Lily looked pointedly at Sarah's breasts, exposed nearly to the nipple in the extravagantly low cut gown, and Sarah flushed and crossed her arms tight against her chest.

"That is it," she declared, spinning on her heel and marching across the bedroom to where her armoire was shoved up against the far wall. "I cannot wear this. I am changing into the dark green dress and—"

"And you will attract exactly zero attention," Lily interrupted, rolling her eyes. "Do not be a ninny. Besides, we do not have any time. The carriage should be here by now."

Just short of distraught, Sarah returned to the mirror one final time, hoping something had changed between her last inspection and this one. Unfortunately, it had not. She still did not recognize the woman staring back at her, nor was she sure she wanted to.

This woman had her eyes lined with kohl and

diamonds in her hair. Her lips were red, her eyes a glittering hazel, and blue sapphires dripped from her ears and throat. Touching the borrowed necklace, Sarah swallowed audibly. "I do not look like me," she whispered.

"That," Lily said as she finished clipping a ruby bracelet to her own wrist, "is exactly the point. If you do not turn heads tonight, I fear there is no hope for any of us. Now pick out a cloak and let us be off."

THE CARRIAGE RIDE to Almack's was blissfully short which was fortunate for the air was bitterly cold and snowflakes had already begun to fall from the night sky. Hugging their cloaks tight around their exposed shoulders, Sarah and Lily hurried inside with Aunt Ingrid trailing behind whom, for once, had put down her book in favor of a brightly colored silk fan.

"These events get inexplicably warm you know," she had said in the carriage, "and I cannot take a nap if I am too hot."

They gave their names to the announcer at the top of the stairs and descended slowly into the mayhem of swirling bodies, raised voices, and half-filled champagne glasses. Spying a friend through the crush of bodies Aunt

Ingrid bid them farewell and wandered off.

"Here," Lily said as she plucked a flute of champagne from a silver tray held out by a passing servant, "drink this. Quickly, before anyone sees."

Sarah, who had never so much as had a sip of port before, eyed the golden bubbles dubiously. "Champagne?" Her nose wrinkled. "Why would I ever do that?"

"Because it will give you confidence. Which you need in spades if everything you told me about your sleigh ride with Lord Heathcliff is true."

"It is," Sarah said miserably. Already feeling rather reckless given her appearance, she plucked the glass from Lily's hand and downed the contents in one hard swallow. "Oh," she said as it slid pleasantly down her throat and pooled in her belly, "that was quite nice."

Lifting one eyebrow Lily gave her an *I told you so look* and held out another glass. "One more and we will do the rounds."

This time Sarah drank the champagne without question. Her limbs felt surprisingly light as they began to make their way through the crowd, and she giggled particularly hard at the sight of Lord Dentham, a man of walrus like proportions, dancing with Lady Griswold, a woman so thin she would have been all but invisible had she stepped behind one of the slender white columns that ran the length of the great ballroom.

When someone jostled her elbow she turned automatically, and her eyes widened in surprise when she saw it was a rather handsome blond haired, blue eyed gentleman. Lily stopped as well, and listened attentively as the man introduced himself.

"Good evening," he said, sinking into a gallant bow that for some reason made Sarah giggle again. "I am Lord Gibson and who might you lovely flowers be?"

"I am Lady Kincaid," Lily said, handling the introductions as she always did, "and this is my close acquaintance, Lady Dawson."

"Lady Dawson," Gibson, savoring the name as if it were a decadent piece of chocolate. His gaze traveled leisurely from the top of Sarah's coiffure to the tips of her dancing slippers, pausing only half a second longer than necessary on her bosom before sweeping back up to her face. "I am absolutely delighted. Is this your debut?"

Rather flustered by the intimate – and by no means subtle – perusal of her body, Sarah missed the question entirely. "My... my what?" she asked.

"Lady Dawson has been traveling until recently," Lily

interceded smoothly. "She has just returned to London."

It was not exactly a lie. Sarah *had* been traveling, if one counted the trip back and forth to her family's estate in the country two months ago. And it was certainly a better answer than the truth: that this was her seventh season and she had yet to attract the attention of a single suitor.

"Might I place my name on your dance card?" Lord Gibson queried with a smile.

Belatedly Sarah realized he had a mustache that curled over the edge of his top lip and was waxed at the corners. It was not a bad mustache – she had certainly seen worse – but she did not find it appealing, and she knew the reason why.

Quite simply, Devlin did not have a mustache.

And his was the only name Sarah wanted on her dance card.

"Sarah, dear," Lily said in a strained voice that was at odds with her beaming smile, "Lord Gibson is awaiting your reply." She lowered her tone and simultaneously raised one hand, feigning a delicate cough while she hissed, "Surely you have heard of Lord Gibson, the *Marquess* of Faraday! If you do not dance with him I shall. Now bat your eyelashes, stick out your chest, and say yes!"

"Yes," Sarah said obediently. She blinked a few times, but it made her feel dizzy, and when she attempted to inexpertly push her chest out something popped in her back. Thankfully Gibson did not seem to notice and, taking her dance booklet, he signed his name with gusto beside the fourth line.

"Until we meet again," he said with great dramatic flair, bowing so low Sarah was quite impressed he did not tip over before he disappeared into the crowd.

"What was that?" Lily cried the moment Gibson was out of sight. Grabbing Sarah's wrist, she stalked past the refreshment tables filled with various pastries, cuts of bread, and colorful fruit to the corner of the ballroom where a handful of fellow wallflowers obligingly turned their heads and feigned deaf ears.

"Have you gone mad?" Sarah asked, yanking her arm free once they were partially obscured behind a towering ivory pillar. The swift walk away from the dance floor had cleared her head immensely, but it had not given her an answer as to why Lily's expressive violet eyes were glittering with annoyance. The brunette's anger did not come as a complete surprise – she was forever getting herself worked up over this and that – although this time

45

Sarah did not have the vaguest clue as to what had caused her temper to flare.

"You hesitated," Lily accused in a hushed tone. Crossing her arms tight across her chest, she tossed back her head and scowled. "When Lord Gibson asked you to dance, you hesitated. Why, Sarah? Any other woman would jump at the opportunity and you had to be talked into it! If this is about Lord Heath—"

"This is not about *him*," Sarah hissed. "And do keep your voice down!" Quickly looking around to ascertain if they had been overhead, she relaxed marginally when she saw the small crowd of wallflowers were more interested in gushing over the arrival of a handsome earl than what she and Lily were arguing about.

"You *promised*," Lily said emphatically. "You gave me your word you would not think of him anymore after the sleigh ride debacle."

With an unhappy sigh Sarah clasped her hands together and looked down, unable to meet Lily's judgmental stare. "I know I did," she whispered. "But I cannot seem to help myself."

"You said he was rude to you," Lily reminded her. "You said he did not even wish you a good day! Is that the kind of man you want to be in love with? No," she

46

said, answering her own question before Sarah could get a word in edgewise. "He is quite nice to look at, I will grant you that. And wealthy, although I know that does not matter to you. But his *demeanor* matters, Sarah. The way he *treats* you matters. And, to be quite honest, he barely knows you are alive."

Sarah flinched from the harsh truth of Lily's words. She knew the point could have been made with more finesse, but then such was not Lily's way. Her friend said what she meant and meant what she said. It was a rare quality and one that Sarah constantly tried to emulate. Around Lily, of course, she was able to speak her mind without stuttering over every other word. But with anyone else – even her own family – she could not help but stammer and blush and forget everything she truly wanted to say. Her exchange with Devlin had certainly proved that.

"You are right," she said softly, even though the admission cost her. "I need to forget him."

"Perhaps you should hold that thought," Lily said, her eyes widening as she gazed over Sarah's right shoulder.

"What?" Certain she had misunderstood her friend, Sarah's brow furrowed in bewilderment as she wondered what could have possibly happened in the span of a few seconds to change Lily's mind so suddenly. "Why?"

"Because Lord Heathcliff has just entered the ballroom… And he is looking right at you!"

CHAPTER FIVE

SARAH'S HEART POUNDED. Lily had not lied. Devlin was, in fact, cutting a swath through the dancers and it appeared as if... but no, he could not be... except he was. He *was* walking straight towards her. Hope, delicate as a bird's wing, fluttered faintly inside of her chest, only to plummet a few seconds later when she realized why the viscount would be approaching them.

"He must want to dance with you again," she said, doing her best to summon a note of excitement in her tone when she wanted nothing more than to bury her head in her hands and cry. She had managed to sit idly by and watch her dearest friend in the arms of the man she loved once, but she knew she would not be able to do it again. Gathering her skirts she began to turn away, but Lily's hand on her arm stopped her.

"You ninny," the brunette said under her breath. "He does not want to dance with me. He is looking at *you*. Now wipe that dumbfounded look off your face and smile! There you go. Very good. I will be right over there if you—"

"Wait," Sarah interrupted with a gasp. Panic stricken, she clung fast to Lily's wrist. "You cannot leave me."

"Would you have him dance with both of us?" Lily gave an amused shake of her head. "You will be fine. Obviously you must have made an impression on him if he is purposefully seeking you out. Just do not stutter. Or be too quiet. Or talk too much."

Sarah's throat tightened. "Lily, I—"

"And whatever you do," her friend continued cheerfully, as if she did not notice that all of the blood had drained from Sarah's face and she was beginning to tremble, "do not step on his feet. Best of luck to you, dear!" she called over her shoulder before she hurried off in a swirl of emerald green skirts, leaving Sarah with nothing more than her worried thoughts as she waited for Devlin to reach her.

She studied him under her lashes as he approached with all the stealthy grace of a panther. There truly was something dangerous about him. Something dark. Something that struck a chord deep inside of Sarah, a chord that reverberated through her entire body, thrumming like a finely tuned bow.

When he finally halted directly in front of her they stared at each other for several long, drawn out moments. She noted his chin and jawline boasted a shadow of hair, as if he had not had time to shave before attending the ball. He looked dashing in black and the sapphire pin stuck through his snowy white cravat brought out the color in his eyes.

"Hello," he said simply.

"Hello," she echoed.

"I had hoped you would be here," he admitted, throwing Sarah completely off guard. She gaped speechlessly at him, unable to think of a single coherent thing to say. He had come to Almack's with the express purpose of finding her? No, surely not. "Since you never told me your name," he continued, his blue eyes glinting with amusement, "I had no way to find you."

"Sarah!" Her tongue darted out to swipe unconsciously at her lower lip and Devlin's gaze lowered, drawn to her lips as a moth to the flame. Hungry desire swept across his face, and her knees wobbled. "My name is Sarah," she finished weakly.

His mouth curved. "Is that what I should call you?" he asked in a husky voice that had her swallowing back a moan. "Sarah? That does not seem very... appropriate.

Are you, Sarah?"

"Am I... Am I what?"

"Appropriate," he whispered. He stepped closer to her, close enough to touch, and touch he did. One arm wound around her waist, his fingertips settling lightly on her hip while the other hand braced on the pillar behind her head, effectively closing her in.

To any curious onlooker his body was angled so it seemed there were yards of space between them, but Sarah felt every one of his breaths as if it were her own, and a thousand horses could not have dragged her eyes from the mole she had just discovered high on his right cheek. It should have been a mar against perfection, but if anything it only served to increase his rugged handsomeness to a level her body was having quite a difficult time adjusting to.

The man, she decided then and there, was the devil himself.

"You may call me L-lady Dawson."

"Is that a question?"

"No," she said, even though it *had* sounded very much like one. "That is my name. Lady Sarah Emily Dawson."

Devlin repeated it in full, lingering on the *Sarah* until she felt her cheeks suffuse with color and she shifted anxiously from side to side. No more than a few minutes in his company and she was already forgetting herself. A lady did not allow a gentleman to call her by her first name. Why, even her mother was always referred to as Lady Dawson, even by her own husband. She had always thought the trait a peculiar one, but now she knew why it existed.

First names were much too intimate. They should be spoken in a private place, like a bedroom... In the bed... Beneath the sheets... Oh dear. Now was *not* the time for her colorful imagination to rear its head. In fact, it was probably the worst time imaginable for her to think of what it would be like to have Devlin stretched out across her naked body, his hands and mouth doing all kinds of naughty things to her damp skin while he moaned her name...

"You may call me Devlin if you wish," the viscount said with a wicked smile, as if he could read her thoughts and was vastly entertained by them. "In fact, I insist on it."

Fairly certain her face was the approximate shade of a tomato in mid-August, Sarah pressed both hands to her warm cheeks in an effort to cool them and shook her head vigorously from side to side. "Oh no," she breathed. "I simply… That would be… No," she said firmly as she struggled to rein in her emotions. She could not afford to lose her head, especially considering she had already lost her heart. "That would simply not do, Lord Heathcliff. Why, we hardly know each other at all and you would do well to remember your manner—"

"Would you care to dance?" he interrupted, holding out his hand. "Once you dance with someone I find you know them much more… intimately than you did before. Surely then it would be reasonable for us to be on a first name basis."

Sarah still stared longingly at his offered hand and almost took it, but her own good manners, instilled to the bone after years of tutoring, stopped her. "My next dance is spoken for," she said regretfully.

Devlin slowly lowered his arm, a smile flirting with the corners of his mouth as though he did not believe her. "Oh really? By whom?"

"Lord…" What was his name? Oh, yes. Now she remembered. "Lord Gibson."

Devlin's eyes flashed unexpectedly, stormy blue and full of temper. "Lord Gibson, the Marquess of Faraday?"

Confused by the sudden change in Devlin's tone and the rigid set of his jaw, Sarah nodded hesitantly. "Do you… Do you know him?" He looked so angry she thought he must, and feared their connection was not a pleasant one.

"Only that his father is ill and by years end he should be a duke."

Sarah had never lost a parent, but she imagined the pain to be quite keen, and she felt instant sympathy for Gibson even though she knew him not at all. "That is quite sad."

"Is it?" Devlin shrugged. "Not for him or his future wife, who will be a duchess." He studied her intently, as if he could see straight through to her very soul, and Sarah, now flustered beyond all bearing, tittered nervously.

"I… I suppose that is true," she said.

Devlin stepped closer, crowding her back against the ivory pillar. She looked down towards his feet, but he cupped her chin and forced her head to lift. "Is that what you want?" he growled. "To be a wealthy duchess, lording over a household full of servants? To have your peers look upon you with envy as you pass? To love a man for what he can give you instead of loving him for who he is?"

"I d-do not know," Sarah gasped. She did not

understand what had caused Devlin's unprecedented fury, nor had she a clue how to subdue it. Tension spread like wildfire from a knot in the middle of her back and trickled up to her shoulders and neck. She fought the urge to jerk away, but like a fox that had its leg caught in a trap she instinctively knew Devlin's grip would only tighten if she tried to pull back. "I could save the fifth dance for you," she offered hesitantly, even though she wasn't quite sure if she wanted to dance with him at all anymore given his current mood.

He studied her a moment longer, those piercing eyes filled with an anger she was helpless to comprehend, before he abruptly released her and spun around. "Go," he said in a short, clipped tone, as if he were dismissing a maid, "and do not bother saving anything for me. I am leaving. There is nothing worthy of my interest here."

Sarah's skin went clammy. Her breath caught in her chest. As she digested the implication behind his cruel remark her mouth opened and closed, but no words came out. There was nothing to say. Except...

"You... You... You..."

"Yes?" Devlin asked calmly, pivoting on one heel and glancing at her sideways with bored resignation, as if he had already forgotten she existed and was annoyed she was wasting more of his time.

"You are horrible!" she burst out in a shrill voice that turned half a dozen heads. "Absolutely horrible!" Immediately she clapped her hand to her lips and gasped, her eyes widening in shock as she realized what she had just said. Amazingly, however, Devlin did not berate her further. If anything, he looked amused.

"Horrible, am I?" One dark eyebrow arched. "Would I be as horrible if I were an earl? What about a marquess or a duke?"

Trembling from head to toe, Sarah shook her head. "I do not know what you talking about," she cried, flinging her arms wide. "You speak in riddles that I do not understand."

"But you do not deny it," he said harshly.

"Deny *what*?"

Devlin's mouth opened. Emotions flickered across his face, emotions that she was helpless to understand. Anger. Need. Hope. Regret. She waited for him to say something, to say *anything*, but with a careless shrug of his broad shoulders he turned and walked away.

CHAPTER SIX

"IT TASTES A-A-AWFUL," Sarah cried, making a face even as she leaned forward to accept the second glass of brandy Lily was holding out. She drank the amber liquid in one hard swallow, sputtered, fought the urge to retch, and lifted the glass again. "Another, please."

Lily crossed her father's study to fetch the entire bottle of fifty year old scotch he kept tucked away in the bottom drawer of his desk and poured them both a liberal shot. Solemn faced, the two women clinked their glasses together and drank.

"That really is awful stuff," Lily gasped as her eyes filled with tears. "But I can certainly see why men drink it. Perhaps we had best let it settle, though, before we have another."

Sarah nodded in silent agreement. After three glasses she was feeling more than a little light headed. Kicking off her dancing slippers, she tucked her legs up and turned in her large, comfortable leather chair to face the fire that was crackling merrily in the hearth. She had only been in Lord Kincaid's study once before, when she and Lily had been caught sneaking out her bedroom window after dark. They had received quite a stern lecture then and she imagined they would get the same treatment now if anyone came home to discover them half drunk and hiding away where they were most definitely not supposed to be.

"Are you certain your parents will not be back tonight?" she asked for the second – or was it the third? – time.

"Positive," Lily said confidently. "The last time they attended a dinner at Lord and Lady Bane's home they did not straggle in until the wee hours of the morning, looking *quite* worse for wear I might add."

"And Elsa?" Sarah asked, referring to Lily's twelve year old sister and renowned tattle tale. She did not bother wasting breath asking about Aunt Ingrid, who had fallen asleep on the carriage ride home and had to be carried inside by a footman.

Lily rolled her eyes. "It is like you do not know me at all. Elsa is fast asleep, and I gave her nanny two extra shillings to make sure she stays that way. You worry too much, Sarah. Just relax, dear, and let the brandy do its work. You have had quite a trying night."

If by 'trying' Lily meant Sarah had been openly humiliated by the man she loved then yes, her night had been *very* trying.

Lowering her head to the armrest, she tucked her hands into the soft folds of the nightgown she was borrowing, closed her eyes, and sighed. The fire played warmly across her face, drying the tears that had continued to fall intermittently from her lashes since Lily had whisked her away from Almack's in a rush following Devlin's direct cut.

"I do not understand what I did wrong," she murmured, opening her eyes in time to see Lily cross in front of the hearth and settle into an adjoining chair.

"You did absolutely nothing wrong," her friend said loyally. Absently combing her long dark hair over one shoulder, she continued, "The fault lies entirely with Lord Heathcliff. Why, the *nerve* of him, giving you the cut like that! He is a beast, Sarah, and you need to forget about him. We shall find you a nice quiet man to marry. One who enjoys reading as much as you do and long walks in the park. Would that not be lovely?"

It sounded wretchedly boring to Sarah, but she did not dare voice her opinion out loud. How could she explain that one of the things that drew her most to Devlin was the fact that he was so *different* from her? She did not *want* to be with someone who was exactly the same as she was. She wanted someone who was adventurous, and spoke their mind, and did not care a whit for what Society thought of them; all things that Devlin was, and she was not.

"Sarah?"

"Hmmm?"

Lily sat up in her chair. "You are thinking about him even now!" she accused.

Sarah flinched. "No," she lied unconvincingly. "I am not."

With a snort of thinly veiled disgust Lily sprang to her feet and began to pace across the length of the study, her long shadow rippling along the bookshelves that lined the walls. She muttered under her breath as she walked, and even though Sarah could not make out complete sentences, she heard the occasional word. "Ridiculous" seemed quite popular, as did "foolish", "asinine", and "hopeless". When Lily finally stopped and turned to face her, arms crossed and face set into a rather formidable expression, Sarah waited for the lecture to begin and nearly fell out of her chair when Lily said:

"There is only one thing left to do, I suppose. You have to marry him."

Certain the brandy was affecting her hearing, Sarah sat bolt upright and hugged her knees to her chest. "Marry... Marry who, Lily?" she asked cautiously.

The brunette rolled her eyes. "Lord Heathcliff, of course."

"And how... how would I accomplish this?"

"The same way a woman always catches a man. You put yourself in a compromising position and force him to offer for your hand."

"A c-compromising position?" she squeaked.

"Although," Lily continued in a thoughtful tone, as if Sarah had not spoken a word, "if he does *not* agree to marry you then you will, of course, be shunned from society and ruined indefinitely. But that is the risk you must be willing to take!"

Sarah was beginning to feel quite queasy. "It is?"

Lily clapped her hands together. "It is."

"Oh, well, I do not really think—"

"Do you love him or not?" Lily said sternly.

"I think I love him, but I—"

"Do you want to be with him or not?"

"I do want to be with him, however—"

Sighing, Lily perched on the edge of Sarah's chair and squeezed her hand. "Look at me. Very good. Now, listen closely. It is no secret that you do not have a single gentleman interested in you and, while *I* personally do not believe twenty and three is that old, the *Ton* has you gathering cobwebs on a shelf. You want a family, do you not?"

When Lily put it *that* way, Sarah was forced to agree. Slowly, hesitantly, she nodded her head.

"And someone to support you?"

At this Sarah frowned. She rather thought the idea of needing a husband to live was an old fashioned one, but she knew she was in the minority. As far as society was concerned a woman's goal in life was simple: find a man with a title and wealth, marry him, and raise a brood of squalling children so their house in the country would pass on to someone other than the crazy uncle.

It was not the most romantic of notions, but Sarah knew her options were limited. Her parents would not be able to support her forever, especially when they had three other daughters between the ages of fourteen and twenty. Her father was a baron, and while he never discussed financial matters with the rest of the family and they lived quite comfortably, Sarah was not oblivious.

She knew her mother had stopped buying new gowns for herself last spring and Julia – the youngest of the four sisters – had a wardrobe contrived of nothing save hand-me-downs from her older siblings.

"Sarah?" Lily prompted, her lips pursing as she waited for an answer.

"Oh very well, I *do* need someone to support me. Although if I had my way it would not be so," she grumbled under her breath.

Lily held up her hand and began to fold down her fingers one by one. "You desire a family, you require financial security, and you must wed before you are a withered up old maid. Have I missed anything?"

"No," Sarah said glumly.

"And you are positively certain you want Lord Heathcliff?"

"I… Well, that is to say yes, I do, although I would need to know why he acted so poor—"

"Do you *desire* Lord Heathcliff?"

In an instant Sarah's cheeks went from pale ivory to burning red. "Lily," she gasped, pulling her hand free and scooting to the edge of the chair. "That is a most inappropriate thing to—"

"I will take that as a yes," the brunette said with

satisfaction. "And if that is the case then it has been decided."

As a recipient of Lily's wayward scheming on more than one occasion, Sarah did not share her friend's enthusiasm. "Lily," she said cautiously, wishing she had not drunk *quite* so much for surely everything would be making much more sense if she were sober, "exactly what has been decided?"

Jumping to her feet, Lily spread her arms wide and grinned like a cat that had just swallowed the proverbial canary. "Why, your marriage to Lord Heathcliff, of course!"

"My m-m-marriage?" Sarah sputtered.

"Granted we can get you two in a compromising situation, of course. *And* he agrees to offer for your hand. *And* he actually goes through with the wedding. *And* you do not end up with your heart broken, shunned by your family and all of society, forced to flee to the coast of France to escape your ruined reputation and take up work as a dockside tart." Lily blinked. "This is one of the best ideas I have ever come up with, I think. Truly, what could go wrong?"

CHAPTER SEVEN

AS IT TURNED OUT, compromising oneself was not as easy as it seemed. For one, it had taken Lily nearly seven days to convince Sarah to go along with her scheming. Eventually she gave in simply to shut Lily up and (although she was loathe to admit it) a small part of her secretly thrilled at the idea of being Devlin's wife, whether it be by fair means or foul.

Once Sarah finally agreed to the plan, they had sought to set it in motion. That was where they ran into their second problem: Devlin could not be found.

For all intents and purposes the viscount had vanished off the edge of the earth. For a week straight Sarah and Lily attended every ball, play, and tea party within London in the hopes of catching sight of him, but it was all to no avail. The man was gone and no one – not even his poor butler, whom Lily had cornered and interrogated – knew where he was.

On the brink of giving up, Sarah agreed to join Lily

for late afternoon tea at Twinings. She went alone, for both her parents were at a museum showing and all three of her sisters were in the midst of their afternoon singing lessons. It was not considered acceptable for a young woman of her station to be out walking alone, but the trek to Twinings was short and she knew once she reached the cozy little tea shop faithful Aunt Ingrid would be there to play the part of chaperon. Dressed to the nines in a thick wool cloak, two scarves, and a fur trimmed hat Sarah set out, navigating the bustling foot traffic as best she could given the precarious footing.

It was now mid-way through December and winter had not been kind to the city. Snow, all but nonexistent last year, had been falling nearly nonstop since early November. As a result the streets were often packed to the gills for where there should have been two traveling lanes there was now only one. Tempers were high, angry words quick to fly. Even the upper class, usually so impervious to the woes of the lower, were beginning to feel the strain of the harsh, unforgiving season.

Keeping her head down and her eyes on the narrow path in front of her, Sarah hurried to Twinings as fast as she dared, loathe to stay out in the frigid air any longer than absolutely necessary.

As she walked her thoughts went to Devlin, as they often did. She wondered where he was and what he was doing. She thought of their last encounter, and visibly winced when she remembered how furious he had become with her. Since then Lily had questioned a few well known gossips and now Sarah at least knew *how* Devlin could become so enraged at the idea of her dancing with Lord Gibson over him, what she did not know was *why*.

While she had been covertly watching him from afar for years, he had not known who she was until a few short weeks ago. How, then, could she provoke so much emotion in him? Having always been quite astute when it came to other's feelings, Sarah knew there had not just been anger in Devlin's eyes when he turned from her. He had displayed regret as well, and a sliver of hope she recognized instantly for it was the same she nurtured within herself.

Did he feel the same pull towards her that she did towards him?

It was not something Sarah could put into words, however many times she tried. Was it destiny? Fate? True love? She did not know. She did not even know if she *believed* in any of those things. All she knew was what she felt.

She had always thought that if Devlin ever realized she existed everything would come together, rather like a fairy tale in its last chapter right before the happily ever after. Now, however, she was more confused than ever before and there did not seem to be a solution in sight, no matter how many different schemes Lily came up with.

Of course, Lily could scheme from sunrise to sundown and it would all come to no avail unless they found where Devlin was hiding. Even though it was a foolish notion, Sarah could not help but feel he was avoiding her. Silly, really. She was nothing to him; another nameless face in a long line of nameless women.

Releasing a long, pent up sigh at *that* rather depressing thought, Sarah tightened her scarf around her neck to ward off the slicing chill of the wind and turned left. Without warning the heel of her boot skidded across a patch of hidden ice. A muffled shriek burst past her lips as she flew up in the air, arms wind milling wildly. With nothing to cushion her fall, Sarah fell hard on her back. Her head slammed into the frozen earth, there was a bright flash of light… and then nothing but darkness.

DEVLIN WATCHED SARAH fall as if from a great distance.

Helpless to save her, he tried to nonetheless, sprinting between two carriages and nearly upending a third. Falling to his knees beside her, his hands flew across her body, gently probing for any broken bones.

People gave them a wide berth as they passed and no one offered to help. A fainting woman was not such an uncommon occurrence, and by the familiar way Devlin was crouched over Sarah no one had any reason to doubt he was not her husband or a close family relative.

He spoke her name once, twice, three times. Her eyelashes fluttered against her pale cheeks, delicate as golden butterfly wings, and Devlin eased her head onto his lap, supporting her neck while she slowly surfaced from unconsciousness.

"What… What happened?" she breathed, blinking in confusion.

"You slipped on the ice and fell. Do not move," he warned when she gasped and struggled to sit up. "I do not believe you have broken anything, but you have quite a knot on the back of your head. My townhouse is a short walk from here. I can carry you there."

Sarah's forehead creased. "D-Devlin?" she asked in bewilderment.

"Yes. I was across the street when I saw you fall." A

half smile curved his mouth as he tucked an errant lock of hair behind her ear. "And that is Lord Heathcliff to you, Lady Dawson. Let us not forget what a stickler you are for propriety."

"Devlin," she repeated, as if he had not spoken a word. And then, in a wondrous voice: "I must be dreaming."

"Do I often appear in your dreams, then?" Grinning, Devlin scooped her up in his arms as if she weighed no more than a sack of feather down. Her head lolled against his chest and she sighed, her eyes drifting closed. Alarmed, he gave her a little shake and her eyes popped open at once.

"Stop that," she complained, glaring up at him. "My head hurts."

"I know darling," he said soothingly. "I know it does. But you cannot fall asleep, do you understand?"

"Cannot fall asleep," she sighed.

"Exactly so."

Devlin could not remember ever walking so fast in his life. Navigating the late afternoon foot traffic with ease, he all but sprinted to his brownstone at the end of the street. Reynolds met him at the door, opening it with his usual timeless precision and watching with carefully concealed interest as Devlin swept inside, still cradling Sarah in his arms as if she were a child.

"I will need a basin of hot water, towels, and a nightgown brought up to my chambers at once," Devlin demanded. "Lady Dawson struck her head on the ice and I fear she may be concussed."

"Should I call a physician?"

He shook his head. "No, I just need what I asked for, and be quick about it Reynolds!" Without waiting for the butler's reply he bounded up the stairs and headed directly for the double oak doors at the end of the wide hallway. Kicking them open with one well placed strike of his boot, he carried Sarah across the master bedroom and laid her ever so gently in the middle of his bed. She moaned as he eased her head back onto one of the pillows, and mumbled something under her breath while he began to unlace her shoes.

"What was that?" Gently easing one shoe off and then the other, Devlin peeled away her stockings as well for they, like the rest of her clothing, had gotten soaked through while she laid on the ground.

"I asked where I was and – Lord Heathcliff!" With something that sounded halfway between a shriek and a squeal, Sarah shot up into a sitting position, her eyes darting wildly around the room before they landed on Devlin. Her mouth dropped open, and as she slowly followed his gaze down to her bare ankles, she shriek/squealed again. "What... How did... I... Oh, oh this is most improper! Lord Heathcliff, *what are you doing here?*"

Devlin enjoyed seeing Sarah when she was so flustered. He had never met another woman who could come undone quite so easily. It was refreshing after being surrounded day in and day out by calculating shrews who manipulated every twitch of emotion that crossed their faces. Sarah was genuine and innocent and good – all things he went out of his way to assume women were not. All things his past experiences *told* him they were not, and yet Sarah proved all of his preconceived notions completely false. He had never been so happy to be wrong in all his life.

Easing away from the edge of the bed he held up his hands, palms facing towards her, and suppressed a grin when she grasped the edge of the top quilt and brought it up to her chin.

"You slipped on the ice and cracked your head. I brought you here, to my townhouse," he explained patiently for the second time.

Sarah's eyes widened. "But w-why would you do that?"

"Why would I help you?" he said, being deliberately obtuse.

"No." Her lower lip jutted out in frustration, and it took all of Devlin's considerable self-control not to take that pouting lip between his teeth and—

"Why would you bring me here? To your home," she clarified, her brows knitting together over the bridge of her nose.

Crossing the room to where a water pitcher rested next to the washbasin, Devlin poured a glass. "A drink?" he asked, holding it aloft. Pressing her lips tightly together, Sarah shook her head from side to side and immediately winced, reminding them both of the seriousness of her injury. "Wait here," he said.

"Where would I go?" Sarah cried after him as he left the room in search of the items he had requested. Reynolds met him at the top of the stairs, red faced and out of breath.

"Here," the butler said, transferring a pile of freshly pressed towels into Devlin's arms. "The water will be done boiling in a minute. I will have it brought up as soon as it is ready. Is there anything else you desire, Lord

Heathcliff?"

Of their own accord Devlin's eyes flicked to the room he had just left and the woman he had left in it. "Reynolds, have you ever apologized to a woman?"

The butler rubbed his moustache. "Apologized to a woman, my lord?"

"Yes. I do not believe I ever have, and I need to know the best way to go about it."

"My wife is always most pleased when I bring her a present. She seems to be particularly fond of jewelry."

Devlin's eyebrows lifted in surprise. "You have a wife, Reynolds?"

"For thirty two years and counting," the butler replied.

"Did I know this?"

"Apparently not, my lord."

"Hmmm..." Devlin shifted the towels to one arm. "Jewelry, you say?"

Reynolds nodded. "Jewelry."

"Do I have any jewelry to give?"

The butler shook his head.

Well that was certainly a problem. Devlin knew he had great strides to cover in making up for the way he had treated Sarah. His behavior had been abominable. He could not remember ever losing his composure like that before, not even with Moira.

Sarah did things to him… She made him feel things he had never felt; to want things he had never wanted. He had no idea how such a quiet, unassuming girl could have such an effect on him after only two encounters; he knew only that she did, and he was helpless against the blossoming of new, uncharted feelings he felt deep inside his chest whenever he thought of her.

"Go down to the jeweler on Elms Street. Bring back the most expensive necklace they have. One with emeralds." Emeralds would bring out the soft flickers of green in her eyes that Devlin doubted she even knew existed. He had never met a woman who was so blissfully unaware of her own natural beauty. "Oh, and Reynolds," he added as the butler began to walk back down the steps.

"Yes, my lord?"

"Things are going to start changing around here. Next week I want you to bring your wife for dinner. Do you have children?"

For the first time Devlin could remember, the butler looked positively flabbergasted. "I… Well, that is to say, yes… Yes I do."

"Excellent. How many?"

"How many?"

"How many children, Reynolds." Devlin rolled his eyes. "Good God man, no wonder you have to buy your wife jewelry. How many children do you have?"

"Three."

"Three children," Devlin mused. He would like children. At least three, he decided on the spot. Three bright eyed, laughing girls with their mother's blond hair and their father's love for horses. "Bring them as well. I want to meet them."

From down the hall came the sound of something crashing and a muffled shout. Devlin spun around. "A necklace, Reynolds!" he called over his shoulder as he raced back to the master bedroom. "With emeralds. Lots of emeralds!"

The butler lingered on the stairs for a moment, watching Devlin until he vanished from sight. Stroking his mustache, Reynolds grinned broadly. It was high time Devlin found love, even though he went about it in the most unconventional of ways.

CHAPTER EIGHT

"I WANT TO GO HOME." Holding the water pitcher above her head in what she hoped was a threatening gesture, Sarah glared daggers at Devlin. "This is most inappropriate. You... You have kidnapped me!"

Devlin took a step closer. Sarah raised the pitcher higher. Her arms trembled from the weight, and he instantly retreated. "Put that down. You are going to hurt yourself."

With a gasp, Sarah released her grip as her elbows gave way. The pitcher sailed through the air towards Devlin, but he ignored it to grab Sarah as she crumpled to the floor. Following suit with the plate she had thrown to get someone's attention, the pitcher shattered against the wall.

"I am sorry," Sarah moaned as Devlin helped her to her feet and eased her back into the bed. She let him arrange her limbs and tuck her under the covers as if she were a doll, too dizzy to complain. "I will replace the pitcher and the plate." Closing her eyes, she turned her face into the pillow. She did not want Devlin to see her like this: weak and cranky as a child.

Sarah had not realized her head injury was so severe until she attempted to get out of the bed and was barely able to make it halfway across the room. Her entire skull was pounding from the inside out, the pain of it enough to cause her eyes to tear and her stomach to turn.

She could not remember anything between slipping on the ice and Devlin carrying her up the stairs. How he had been the one to find her was a complete mystery, as was *why* he had insisted on bringing her back to his home. It was ironic, really.

For two weeks she had spent every waking moment wondering where he was, and then suddenly – as if by magic – he had appeared when she needed him most. Except (quite selfishly) she wished their third meeting had not been under such unflattering circumstances. Soaked through the skin with an enormous lump on her head was hardly the way to make a good impression, nor, she admitted silently, was throwing a plate across the room. Perhaps that had been a bit extreme, but Sarah had panicked when she realized the implications that could arise from Devlin bringing her back to his house.

Surely someone had seen them, and surely that someone would tell another someone until it spread like wildfire through the *Ton* and her reputation was completely, irrevocably ruined.

Of course that had been the original plan: to be caught in a situation that would force Devlin's hand in marriage. But now... Now she did not want to *force* him into anything. If he loved her she wanted him to love her, and if he did not... well, then he did not. At least either choice would be of his own volition and not something falsely created by nefarious means, which made her current situation quite problematic.

She was too weak to leave on her own, but if she called for her parents to come get her there would surely be questions asked and answers demanded. That left only one person in the entire world whom Sarah trusted enough to rescue her from her current predicament; unfortunately that was also the only person in the entire world who would be happy she was in it.

No, for once she could not rely on Lily's guidance. She would have to sort it through on her own, and that knowledge alone was enough to send another dizzying wave of pain sweeping over her, so fierce it caused her teeth to clench and her hands to ball into small fists on top of the quilt. She heard Devlin murmur something, and then a warm cloth was pressed gently on her forehead.

"This should help with the headache," he said quietly.

Opening her eyes, Sarah turned to face him, focusing on his worried blue eyes as he leaned over her, his hands braced on either side of her body. "Why are you being so… so nice to me?"

Devlin's broad shoulders lifted and fell in a quick shrug. "Because I was rude to you before. On both occasions," he admitted with a wayward smile that did something sinfully delightful to her insides.

Holding the warm cloth in place – it *did* feel quite good – Sarah leaned up on one elbow. As obliging as a well-trained nurse Devlin automatically fluffed a pillow to put behind her shoulders and she sagged against it gratefully. "You were rather rude," she said shyly, lowering her gaze to the flower pattern sewed into the quilt.

"Which is why I shall do my best to make up for it now. Is there anything else you need? A glass of water? Something to eat?"

Embarrassingly cognizant of her damp dress and tangled hair – her cloak and hat must have been lost somewhere along the way – Sarah nibbled on her bottom lip as she thought of the best way to phrase her next question.

"I can have a maid draw up a bath for you," Devlin said, his smile turning rather impish as Sarah blushed. "And find a change of clothing as well. Arrangements have already been made. You can stay here for as long as you wish."

Her eyes flew to his in startled alarm. "Oh, no, I could not impo—"

"You are not fit to leave this room, let alone walk home. Not to mention, we are in the midst of a snow storm."

"A… A snowstorm?"

There was an undeniable hint of smug satisfaction in Devlin's tone as he crossed the room and drew back the curtains.

Sitting up a little straighter and squinting, Sarah could just make out a flood of white falling with alarming intensity from the sky. Everything in sight was covered; the roads not even clearly visible. Traveling home, even if she did not have a pounding headache, would be nigh on impossible until the weather cleared.

Her shoulders drooping in defeat, Sarah sagged back against the pillows. "I suppose a hot bath would be very nice."

Leaving the curtains open, Devlin turned to face her and crossed his arms, a faint smile capturing the corners of his mouth. "I will have one readied for you immediately."

Not trusting the mischievous glint in his eye, Sarah said, "Of course it will be a very *private* bath."

"Of course," he agreed readily.

"And the change of clothing…"

"You will have your choice of nightgowns and robes." At Sarah's raised brow, he chuckled. "Very *high* necked nightgowns and robes fit for a grandmother. Not to worry. You shall be covered head to foot. I can assure you, Lady Dawson, I am not as much of a scoundrel as you seem to think I am."

Saying nothing, Sarah merely pursed her lips.

"Well, perhaps I am a bit of a scoundrel. But nothing the right woman could not fix." On that rather enigmatic note, he left the room. Through the closed door Sarah heard him requesting hot water to be drawn and the claw foot tub in the corner of the master bedroom, half concealed by a silkscreen, to be filled.

Telling herself she would only doze until it was ready, Sarah closed her eyes… and fell instantly asleep.

WHEN SHE WOKE the room was dark save the flickering light that danced out from a fire someone had started in the hearth. Staring at the flames helped Sarah remember where she was, for her family was not so wealthy they had fireplaces in every room, let alone the master bedroom.

The throbbing in her skull had subsided to a dull ache, and when she gently touched the lump on the back of her head she was relieved to discover the swelling had already begun to subside. That would make going home in the morning all the more easier – as long as the weather cooperated.

Grasping the edge of the blankets, Sarah tossed them aside and swung her legs over the side of the bed. That was when she could not help but notice she was *not* wearing the dress she had fallen asleep in.

The pale blue nightgown was made of the softest cotton she had ever felt against her bare skin. It was quite beautiful, with delicate ivory lace along the neckline, and very modest as well, just like Devlin had promised – although he had not said anything about getting her changed in her sleep!

A piece of parchment on the nightstand caught her

eye. The scrawl was unfamiliar, but she instinctively knew it was Devlin's handwriting even before she read his signature at the bottom.

If you are reading this, it means you are
awake. Ring the bell, no matter the hour.
If you require assistance. I will be
there at once. Yours fondly,
Devlin

Sarah reread the short note twice, then once more for good measure, seeking some
hidden nuance that would tell her the viscount's hidden thoughts. If she did not know any better she would say he was attempting to woo her. The signs were certainly there: whisking her away to his private residence, putting her in his very own bedroom, caring for her every whim, speaking to her kindly – no, *flirtatiously* – at every turn. She strummed her fingers against her chin as she considered the small silver bell he had left beside the note. There was nothing she *required*, per say. She was a bit hungry, but could easily wait until breakfast. She had no reason in the world to ring the bell. Except…

Except maybe want was reason enough.

She was not some wide eyed, blushing schoolgirl. Well, perhaps she *was* rather prone to blushing, but she was most definitely not a girl. She was a woman full grown. A woman who had never known the touch of a man. The feel of a man's mouth sliding across her neck... The rough texture of a man's hands as he grasped her hips... The husky murmur of a man's voice as he whispered all of the decadent things he wanted to do to her…

And why *shouldn't* she know those things? If she was going to be ruined, she might as well make certain she was ruined thoroughly.

Before she gave herself time to come to her senses, Sarah's hand shot across the nightstand and she rang the bell.

CHAPTER NINE

THE SECONDS THAT passed between the time she rang the bell and Devlin knocked at the door were the longest of Sarah's life. Uncertain whether she should be in the bed or out, she hovered at the foot of it, her fingers twisting anxiously behind her back while she fought to steady her breathing.

At the sound of a hand rapping softly against the door she jumped like a startled doe and had to clear her throat twice before she managed to croak, "Come in."

Devlin slipped into the room. The fire cast his profile into shadow, but there was enough light for Sarah to see he had changed clothes as well. His white linen shirt was unbuttoned at the collar and rolled up at the cuffs, as though he had been working before she summoned him. A lock of dark hair curled over one eye, giving him a rakish appearance, and as he stepped towards her he swept it back with an impatient flick of his wrist.

"You are awake." His gaze swept down her body, studying her as intimately as she had just studied him, and Sarah fought the maidenly urge to cover herself. "How do you feel?"

"I… Much b-better. I feel much better." Sarah took a step back and bumped into the mattress. Wrapping one hand around the carved mahogany bedpost to steady herself, she managed what she hoped was an entrancing smile and said, "Thank you for helping me. I do not know what would have h-happened if you had not come along."

Devlin shook his head. "There is no need to thank me. I hope you do not mind, but I had one of the maids change you out of your dress. I did not want you to catch a chill from sleeping in damp clothing. I can even give you my word I was not in the room at the time."

"Did you want to be?"

"Did I want to be what?"

Feeling as though a thousand butterflies were dancing in her belly, Sarah bit her lip and blurted, "In the room."

Devlin's eyes widened ever so slightly and for once he was the one who stuttered. "I… That is to say… Is there anything you need, Lady Dawson?"

It was now or never. Looking Devlin straight in the eye, Sarah drew a deep, steadying breath even as her knees trembled and her heart threatened to beat right out of her chest. "You," she whispered. "I need you."

This time there was no mistaking the Devlin's shock at Sarah's forwardness. His entire body stiffened and he took one step towards her before he stopped himself, jaw clenching tight. "Lady Dawson, you do not know what you are saying."

Now that she had admitted her deepest, darkest desire Sarah felt as if a great weight had been lifted from her shoulders. Of their own accord her feet began to move, carrying her purposefully across the room. As he watched her approach Devlin's arms remained rigid at his sides, the only sign he was having difficulty controlling himself in the clenching and unclenching of his fists.

Tipping her chin up Sarah studied the fathomless depths of his stormy blue eyes and what she saw caused her lips to curve and an unprecedented sense of confidence to settle serenely on her shoulders.

"Call me Sarah." She raised her hands and pressed them flat against Devlin's chest. He inhaled sharply at her touch, and her smile grew. Through the thin fabric of his shirt she could feel his heartbeat. It thundered under her palms, revealing Devlin was not quite as composed as he would have her believe. "And I know exactly what I am saying."

"Sarah…" He spoke her name on a ragged breath, his expression pained as he gazed down at her. "Are you certain? I do not want you to regret—"

She rose up on her tiptoes and pressed her mouth to his, effectively silencing him. For a fleeting moment he did not move, and she hesitated, suddenly unsure if she had been mistaken in her assumption that he desired her as much as she did him, but then on a muffled groan his arms closed around her slender body and he pulled her into his embrace.

For Sarah, whose only experience with kissing came from what she had heard whispered at tea parties and balls, the sensation of having Devlin's lips contoured to hers was blissfully new and exciting. She had no idea what to do, but he guided her patiently, running his tongue along her bottom lip, nibbling at the corners of her mouth, and – surprises of all surprises – kissing *inside* her mouth.

His hands moved in soothing strokes up and down her spine, slipping lower and lower with every pass. Instinctively Sarah moved closer to him, pressing her body tight against his and winding her fingers up through his hair.

Firelight bathed them, flickering over their joined silhouette as Devlin easily scooped her up and carried her to the bed. He laid her upon the mattress with reverence, his gaze boldly traveling the length of her delicate frame before he stretched out beside her, wrapping one arm around her ribcage while the other cupped the back of her head.

"Relax," he whispered against her ear before he lowered his head to nip at the exposed curve of her neck. Sarah shuddered, then sighed with pleasure as he pressed his mouth to hers and drew her tongue to his. "You taste like honey." The hand at her waist began to slowly wander up towards the swell of her breasts. He cupped one and then the other, his thumb flicking over her hardened nipples through the soft cloth of her nightgown while she arched her back and gasped in wonder at the feelings he was bringing to life inside of her, as if she were a violin and he a musician, plucking notes from her body she had never known even existed.

With a deft pull Devlin undid the laces at the top of her nightgown, baring her shoulders and breasts to his hungry gaze. "Beautiful," he murmured as his fingers trailed over her creamy flesh, leaving goosebumps in their wake. "Perfect." When his mouth followed his fingers Sarah's eyes flew open in shock and quickly darkened with pleasure. She was burning from the inside out, her body aching for someone she could not put into words.

As Devlin teased her nipples with his tongue her hands began to explore the rest of his body. She trailed her fingertips with cautious excitement down between his shoulder blades, her nails digging into his skin until she felt the muscles bunch and quiver. Gaining confidence she reached further, skimming down across his sides and over the flat plane of his stomach. She felt the button on his trousers, cool and hard against her flesh, and – determined to give as good as she was getting – slipped her hand inside.

"Oh God," Devlin rasped out as her fingers tentatively brushed the length of his manhood.

"I am sorry." Sarah's hand retreated as if she had been burned, but on a throaty groan he captured her wrist and wrapped her palm around the hard, hot length of him. She stroked his cock slowly, unsure of how much pressure to apply or even where exactly to touch, but if Devlin's ragged breathing was any indication she was not doing too poor of a job.

The power of bringing him pleasure was a thrill unto

itself and Sarah grew heady with it until Devlin twisted his hips abruptly away. He braced his arms on either side of her head, his strained expression tainted with disbelief.

"Are you certain you are a virgin?" he gasped.

Perhaps it was not the most romantic of questions, but Sarah chose to take it as a compliment. "Quite sure," she said, her lips curving, and Devlin captured her mouth for another lusty kiss that left her breathless and a bit dazed by the time he reared back and stripped away her nightgown, leaving her bare to his gaze.

For a moment she was self-conscious and her arms crept down of their own accord to cover her breasts while heat bloomed across her chest. Devlin merely shook his head and gently pulled her hands away, placing them on his now naked shoulders, for he had removed his own clothes as well, a fact that was contributing to the blush that spread like wildfire across Sarah's collarbone and neck.

"Never hide yourself from me," he ordered sternly, his eyes flashing blue black in the flickering light.

Sarah worried her bottom lip. "I… It is just—"

"I want to look at you. I *need* to look at you." And so began an exploration of her body so thorough, so tantalizingly erotic, that Sarah was quite mindless by the time Devlin was finished. He left no inch of skin untouched. His hands were everywhere, his mouth quick to follow.

When one finger gently slipped through her curls down *there* she went stiff as a board, relaxing only when he whispered sweet assurances and began to stroke her as she had stroked him, and oh, how different it felt to be the one receiving pleasure. It rolled over her in waves, intensifying as his finger slipped *inside* of her, gentle at first, before quickening in pace and depth until she arched off the mattress and cried out his name.

But everything Sarah had felt thus far was nothing... *nothing...* compared to the electricity that jolted through her body when his lips replaced his finger and his tongue lapped at the core of her. He nibbled, licked, and teased while she writhed, tossing her head from side to side and tangling her fingers in his dark hair.

At last, only when Sarah was all but begging for something she could not put into words, did Devlin lift his head and stretch up the length of her body. He adjusted himself smoothly on top of her, and then he was *in* her, pressing ever so steadily into the tight, narrow recess of her womanhood, whispering soothingly into her ear, stroking her hair, her arms, her breasts.

The pain was minimal; a quick burning sensation that vanished as quickly as it had appeared for he had prepared her body with expert finesse. She was ready for him. Wet for him. Crying out for him. They began to move in a sinuous rhythm, thrusting and receiving, giving and taking, gasping and pleading, until, in perfect unison, they sought their release together.

CHAPTER TEN

THE NEXT MORNING Lily came to call.

With Sarah relaxing in the bath and the entire staff delayed by the storm that had buried London in snow overnight, it was left to Devlin to answer the incessant knocking. He did so with a grimace and a grumble, pulling a shirt over his head seconds before flinging the door wide and glaring daggers at the brunette waiting on the other side.

"This had better be an emergency," he snapped.

"Oh, it is," Lily assured him before she swept past without waiting for an invitation, trailing snow in her wake. Swinging her cloak off her shoulders she held it out to Devlin as if he were the butler. He took it grudgingly, as well as the hat, gloves, and muff that followed.

Dumping everything rather unceremoniously in the nearest chair, he wiped his hands dry on the sides of his trousers, crossed his arms, and waited for an explanation.

Lily took her time with it. She wandered in a circle around the large foyer, studying everything from the ornate chandelier that hung from the vaulted ceiling to the collection of crystal ducks – Devlin had a secret fondness for the odd little animal – that were perched high on a shelf. Only when she had completed her circuit did she finally turned to address him.

"Sarah is here," she said without preamble.

"Yes," Devlin acknowledged with an annoyed dip of his head. He recognized Lady Kincaid now that she was divested of her outer garments. She had been with Sarah in the park, and then again at the ball. He thought he might have even danced with her once, but he could not be certain. How she had tracked her friend here he had no idea, but he was quite eager for her to leave. Unfortunately, she did not seem in any great hurry.

"Sarah spent the night here," Lily continued, lifting one eyebrow.

"Yes."

"Did she spend the night with you?"

Devlin gritted his teeth. "I believe you know the answer to that question or you would not be here this morning. What do you want, Lady Kincaid?"

The brunette snapped her shoulder blades together and

lifted her chin. "Do not try bullying *me*, Lord Heathcliff. I am not like Sarah—"

"I never bullied her!" Devlin interrupted with a scowl.

"Oh no? What would you call that little incident at Almacks?"

How his quiet, shy little Sarah and this brash, rude woman were friends was an absolute mystery. Taking a deep, steadying breath to calm himself, Devlin said, "That was a mistake. One I have already apologized for, not that it concerns you."

"*Everything* about Sarah concerns me, including her current welfare. Where is she? I want to see her." Without waiting for his permission Lily shouldered past and marched up the stairs, Devlin hot on her heels.

"Stop this instant," he demanded, but she waved him off.

"Sarah!" she called out, raising her voice so she could be heard above Devlin's blustering. "Sarah darling, can you hear me?"

The door to the master bedroom opened and Sarah, dressed in nothing save a white robe with her wet hair in tangles around her face, peeked out. "Devlin, what is happen—LILY!" she gasped, clapping one hand over her mouth. "What in the world are you *doing* here?"

"Exactly what I want to know," Devlin growled.

Seemingly nonplussed by her friend's lack of clothing, Lily all but flew down the hallway and squeezed Sarah in a tight embrace that left them both breathless. "I had to come see if you were alright, or if that man—" she paused to point an accusing finger at Devlin "—had done something horrid to you."

"Now see here," Devlin protested. "Sarah has come to no harm, in fact she…. Well, she…" Realizing too late he had been about to make a regrettable blunder, Devlin cut himself off as both women pivoted to face him and raised their eyebrows in unison.

"In fact she… What, Devlin?" Sarah asked in a deceptively sweet voice. "Do go on. Finish your sentence."

He looked down at the floor and cleared his throat. "I would rather not."

"Why Sarah, I do believe he is blushing!" Lily said with delight. "Oh, how the tables have turned. Let us get you dressed, dear, and you can tell me all about it."

When Sarah glanced helplessly at him over her shoulder as Lily all but shoved her back into the bedroom, Devlin shook his head and rolled his eyes. Sarah smiled, as if to say, *'What would you have me do?'*

and the exchange, though small and silent, warmed Devlin's heart.

He knew now, beyond a shadow of a doubt, that what he once felt with Moira had been nothing more than a young man's lust. It had certainly not been love. No, love was what he felt when he gazed upon Sarah.

He loved it when she blushed – which he had taken particular delight in making her do this morning – and he loved it when she got that little stutter in her voice. He loved how sweet she was, and how kind. He loved how trusting she was, and how honest. Last night they had hidden nothing from each other and Devlin had never felt closer to another human being in his entire life. She was his match, in every sense of the word, and if he had one regret it would only be that he had overlooked her for so long.

As a plan began to form in Devlin's mind, he bounded down the stairs to make the necessary preparations, leaving Lily and Sarah to their gossip of which he could only hope showed him in the best possible light for he suspected – and rightly so – that if Lady Kincaid did not approve of him it would be an uphill battle to win Sarah's heart.

INSIDE THE MASTER BEDROOM, Lily reclined belly down on the bed while Sarah combed out her long hair and began to plait it into a braid.

At first Sarah had been reserved in sharing details of her heavenly night spent in Devlin's arms, but after enduring a barrage of merciless questions she had finally caved in and, blushing head to toe, gave Lily a full report on what had occurred, leaving no detail left unspoken.

Her friend listened with rapt attention, interrupting every once in a while with little gems such as, "he did *what*?" and "oh, I would have positively *died*" and (Sarah's personal favorite) "I am going to faint".

When she was finally finished recanting her first experience with lovemaking, Sarah sat on the bed beside Lily and wrapped her arms around her knees. "And then we did it all over again this morning," she confessed.

Lily clapped a hand to her forehead. "And here I was worried you were being taken advantage of." Sitting up, she rearranged her skirts and crossed her legs at the ankle. "You little minx, *you* seduced *him*! Sarah Emily Dawson, I never thought I would see the day. How do you feel this morning?"

"Wonderful." Sarah smiled. "Absolutely wonderful."

"And when is the big day?"

"The big day?"

Lily rolled her eyes. "The wedding, you ninny. When are you getting married? Why, even now you could be, you know," she paused to look pointedly at Sarah's stomach, "*in the family way*. There really is no time to waste."

Sarah's smile faltered. "I… We… That has not been discussed yet."

"That has not been *discussed* yet? What is there to discuss! He ruined you, thus he has to marry you."

"He did not *ruin* me," Sarah protested, even as a seedling of doubt in the back of her mind said otherwise. She and Devlin had yet to talk about the future, but she had naturally assumed he would offer for her hand. Now she was suddenly not so certain. Perhaps last night had not meant to him what it meant to her. After all, he'd probably had a thousand of those nights with a hundred different women. How was she any different? *Why* would she be any different? Because she loved him? Sarah winced at the thought.

She did not know if love meant anything to Devlin, let alone if he even loved her or would be capable of loving her. In the light of day it was easy to see how much of a fool she had been. A silly, presumptuous fool who never learned from her mistakes and now may have made the most grievous one of all.

"I have to speak with him," she decided. Leaving the bed, she picked up her clothing that had dried in front of the fire overnight and began to dress herself while Lily watched, worried concern marring her pretty face. "Help me with the stays," she implored, and Lily stood at once, crossing the room and tightening the back of Sarah's dress with four quick pulls.

"Everything will be fine," Lily assured her, although she could not quite keep the doubt from creeping into her tone that Sarah could hear clear as a bell.

"You said it yourself." She fretted anxiously with the end of her braid. "He ruined me, Lily."

"Ah yes, well, perhaps that was a poor choice of words."

"What if he never wants to see me again?"

"Darling, of *course* he wants to see you. He *loves* you. I saw it on his face the moment I walked through the door. I was merely being cautious. You know how I can be. Why, I bet at this very moment he is planning out his proposal."

"No." Sarah shook her head and began to pace. "No, he is not. Why, by now he has probably forgotten my name. What am I going to do, Lily? I w-wanted this to happen but I never thought it would *really* happen."

Unbeknownst to either woman, the bedroom door creaked open.

"Sarah?" Devlin asked uncertainly, stepping into the room and taking in the harried scene. "What is it? What is wrong?"

Lifting tear drenched eyes to his, Sarah choked back a sob, shot past him, and fled.

In the deafening silence that followed her abrupt retreat, Devlin rounded on Lily with a snarl. He had never shaken a woman, but he was sorely tempted to now, especially after witnessing the naked pain he had seen flash across Sarah's face. The urge to help her, to protect her, was like a live thing inside of him, clawing to get free. "What the hell did you say to her?" he demanded.

Helpless to explain, Lily could only shake her head.

On a vicious oath, Devlin spun on his heel and bolted out of the room.

CHAPTER ELEVEN

SARAH MADE IT through the front door before she came up short and nearly flew off the front steps in amazement at the sight that greeted her. There, in the middle of the empty snow covered street, stood Devlin's gray horse and sleigh.

Both had been resplendently decked out in lavish red bows, ornate gold bells, and – even though she had to squint to make them out – sprigs of mistletoe tied together with silver ribbon.

"Do you like it?" Devlin murmured from behind her. "I was coming upstairs to get you. I wanted it to be a surprise."

Sarah startled slightly as Devlin draped her cloak – forgotten in her rush to flee – over her shoulders. "Thank you," she said absently, still distracted by the sleigh and the possible implications of what such a grand gesture could mean.

Coming to stand beside her, Devlin gently took her

hand, his long fingers wrapping easily around her smaller ones. "Come on a ride with me?"

She hesitated. "Devlin, there is something I need to ask—"

"Come on a ride with me," he repeated.

This time it was not a question.

Arm in arm they walked down the steps. The gray horse waited patiently while Devlin first helped Sarah into the sleigh before he went around to the other side and climbed in himself. A flick of the reins, a cluck of his tongue, and they were off, moving with a swift speed Sarah was more accustomed to the second time around.

The wind whistled past her cheeks and caught the hood of her cloak, nearly causing it to fall from her head before she pulled it more firmly down around her ears. Wordlessly Devlin reached down underneath the seat and pulled out the fur blanket he had given her before. This time he used it to cover them both and their thighs brushed intimately as the sleigh moved briskly down the street and turned left, towards the park.

Sarah's heart pounded, so loud she feared Devlin would surely hear, but when she sneaked a sideways glance at his profile she saw his attention was firmly fixed on the winding path in front of them.

Taking a deep breath she settled into the seat and forced herself to relax and enjoy the scenery. Now that they were beyond the houses and shops of the city it passed by in flashes of green and white, so pristine and clear it made Sarah smile despite the aching in her heart. Winter may have been many things, but ugly it was not, at least not in the typical sense of the word.

Despite the frigid temperatures and the ice and bone chilling wind there was a loveliness to all of it that many people failed to realize. There was a sense of magic as well, a soft tingling in the air that made one appreciate their surroundings far more than usual. It filled Sarah with awareness, not just for the beauty of a solitary pine standing guard over a field painted in white, but for herself as a woman.

For the first time she recalled the wish she had made in the darkened study with only Lily to bear witness. A wish that had, for all intents and purposes, come true threefold since its making.

I wish Devlin would simply notice me.

Sarah glanced at him again and this time he was looking back at her, his blue eyes calm and soft with an emotion she dared not name. He eased the horse down to a shuffling walk, shifted the reins to his left hand, and raised the right to gently cup her cheek. She leaned into the pressure, closed her eyes, and sighed.

"You are not a great beauty," he said huskily.

Sarah's eyes shot open. "What d-did you say?" she said, her forehead creasing. She would have drawn back, but he had begun tracing the curve of her jaw with his thumb, and she was too weak a creature to deny herself such a simple pleasure.

"The other women I have been with were all great beauties. Their hair was more golden than yours, their lips more red, their bodies more voluptuous." Here Devlin paused and Sarah, who had grown more and more incredulous with every word he spoke, finally jerked free of his grasp and wedged herself into the farthest corner of the seat she could reach.

"If you are trying to pay me compliments you are not doing a very good job!"

"Oh," Devlin, his blue eyes gleaming and his dimples flashing, "I am paying you the greatest compliment of all. These women," he continued, apparently oblivious to the fact that Sarah did *not* want to hear of anyone else he had been with, "were so beautiful it often pained me to look upon them, for I knew beneath their glittering smiles and batting eyelashes they were as cold and empty as porcelain dolls. They could not love another, you see, for they were already in love with themselves. I knew this, and in knowing it pursued them all the more, for I did not seek love, I sought beauty and all the coldness it brought with it."

"But... But why?" Sarah asked.

"Because when you are cold you cannot feel alive, and when you are not alive you cannot feel love." With a soft murmur Devlin eased down to a full halt. Securing the reins he turned to Sarah and gently drew her hands into his, his fingers tracing across the delicate bumps of her knuckles as he gazed earnestly into her eyes. "But I do not feel cold around you, Sarah. I feel alive, as I have not in years. I loved another once, and when she broke my heart I swore never to open myself to such pain again."

It was beginning to dawn on Sarah that Devlin was trying to tell her how much he cared for her, albeit in a rather roundabout way. She drew in a deep, trembling breath and tried to still the hope that quivered wildly within her breast.

Hope had not served her well in the past, and she dared not set it free now, not when there was still a chance her heart could shatter as surely as Devlin's had all those years ago. "What are you trying to say?" she pressed, searching his eyes for the answer to the most important question of all.

"What am I trying to say?" Devlin repeated wryly. Before she could brace herself he had his arms around her waist and she was whisked into his lap. Stifling her gasp of surprise with a quick brush of his mouth against hers, he cradled her against his chest as if she were made of the finest glass and whispered in her ear, so soft as to barely be heard, "I love you."

"You… You love me?"

"And I want to marry you."

Her jaw dropped. "You want to *marry* me?"

"Yes, you silly girl." Stroking his fingers through her hair, he loosened the knot that held her braid in place and began to unwind the sections tendril by golden tendril. "I loved you from the first moment I saw you, even though I was too proud to admit it. I loved you on that first sleigh ride when you were so delightfully nervous you could barely speak a word, and I shall love you to the last one when we know each other so well no words will need to be spoken. You are my light, Sarah Mine. My heart. My love." He punctuated each declaration with a kiss to her cheek, his lips chasing away the tears that fell like sparkling diamonds from her lashes. "Do not cry," he murmured, pulling her even closer. "You should be happy, not sad."

Tipping her head back Sarah gazed up at him through her tears and managed a choked laugh. "I *am* happy," she assured him. "Happier than I ever dared to be."

He nodded. "Good. Now tell me you love me as well."

"I love you as well," she said obediently.

Devlin's brow furrowed. "That did not sound very convincing."

Clasping her arms around his neck, Sarah squeezed him to her as tight as she could. "I love you." She kissed his chin. "I love you." She kissed the tip of his nose. "I love you."

Devlin frowned. "You missed a spot," he said, pointing to his mouth.

"Did I?" Sarah blinked innocently. "Well, I shall have to fix that."

"At once," he said.

"At once," she agreed.

Laughing, the two lovers clung to each other in an embrace so passionate that for a moment, a moment so quick if you blinked it would be missed, the sun shone a bit more brightly and the snow, for the first time all winter, began to thaw.

THE
RISQUE
RESOLUTION

A Regency Holiday Novella

JILLIAN EATON

The Risque Resolution is a work of fiction. Names, characters, places and incidents are either the product of the author's imagination or are used fictitiously, and any resemblance to actual persons, living or dead, business establishments, events, or locales is entirely coincidental.

© 2014 by Jillian Eaton

CHAPTER ONE

Kincaid Country Residence
Devonshire, England

37 days until Christmas

"LET ME MAKE sure I understand you clearly." Sucking in a deep breath, Lily Kincaid pinched the bridge of her nose and fought the urge to scream. "Due to a clause in Father's will, I must marry before the year is out or everything we own will be given to Cousin Eustace?"

Mr. Guthridge, the Kincaid's lawyer for the better part of two decades, bobbed his head and rattled the paper he held in his hand.

A short, stout man with an impressive salt and pepper moustache and a propensity for stuttering, he looked as though he would rather be anywhere else in England than where he currently was: standing in the middle of the late Lord Kincaid's study delivering the worst news imaginable to his eldest daughter. "Y-yes, I am afraid s-so. Your f-father made it quite clear before his p-passing that in order to receive your inheritance in full you will need to marry."

"Before this year's Christmas," Lily clarified, her violet eyes narrowing.

"Yes," Guthridge confirmed miserably. "That does seem to be the case."

Unable to remain still, Lily began to pace the length of the narrow study. Her skirts moved in an agitated swirl of green between her ankles before she abruptly stopped in front of the window, braced her arms against the sill, and peered out across the back lawn.

Courtesy of a storm that had swept through two days before, the shrubbery surrounding the Kincaid's tidily kept country estate was blanketed in a layer of fresh, powdery snow. Morning light reflected off the skeletal branches of a towering oak, its limbs heavy in winter slumber. Icicles, glistening bright as diamonds, clung to the wooden fence line that wrapped around the edge of the lawn. The very same fence line, Lily thought absently, that her father had been planning to repair before he passed away peacefully in his sleep at the not so advanced age of four and fifty.

For three months Albus Kincaid had been promising

his wife he would fix the fence, but something or other had always come up. A new invention to create. A new discovery to unearth. A new recipe to learn. Albus had been a loving father and husband, but he'd never been a practical man, not in life nor, it seemed, in death.

"Mother is not going to like this," she murmured under her breath.

"What was that?" Guthridge asked.

Lily turned and leaned against the window, letting the chill from the glass cool a rising temper that had nothing to do with the man standing in front of her and everything to do with the one who had placed her in this rather unfortunate predicament. "Was my father of sound mind when he dictated the will? Because if he was not of sound mind then—"

But Guthridge was already shaking his head before she had even completed her sentence. "I am afraid, Lady Kincaid, that your father was of *very* sound mind. He even wrote a letter" – the lawyer paused while he rummaged through his leather satchel before removing a square piece of parchment – "saying exactly that. Would you like to read it?"

Read one of the last things her father wrote before he died? Lily, who had not shed a single tear during the funeral or the three days since while her mother and younger sister wept buckets by the hour, felt her throat inexplicably tighten. "I… No," she managed before she spun around and once again faced the window. "No, Mr. Guthridge, I… I believe you."

"Very well, Lady Kincaid," the lawyer said quietly. "If there is nothing else, I will leave all of the documents on your father's desk for you to examine at your leisure. Although, I pray you do not take much time, for my next visit shall be to your cousin's house."

"My cousin?" Lily said blankly.

Guthridge cleared his throat. "I am afraid so. As he will be the main benefactor if you do not marry within the time allotted, he must be made privy to the will's contents."

Lily let her forehead fall against the glass with a dull *thud*. "What is the date, Mr. Guthridge?"

"The eighteenth of November," the lawyer answered promptly.

"Thirty seven days," she whispered.

"What was that?"

"Thirty seven days," she repeated as she turned around. "I have thirty seven days to find a suitable match, convince him to marry me, and save my family from financial ruin." She smiled weakly. "You are not in the business of giving out Christmas miracles, are you Mr. Guthridge?"

Looking more uncomfortable now than ever before, the lawyer shook his head. "I am afraid not. But perhaps with the help of your mother—"

"Oh no." The very idea was enough to cause Lily to cringe. "Mr. Guthridge, I realize this is a bit unorthodox, but you must promise not to tell my mother about the will's conditions. It will send her into a panic," she continued hastily when the lawyer opened his mouth, "and right now she is so distraught I fear more bad news would be very ill advised. She loved my father very much, you see, and his death... Well, his death has been hard on all of... on all of us."

There were those blasted tears again. They had a habit of sneaking up when she least expected them, no matter how hard she tried to keep them at bay. It was not that she did not *want* to cry. It was just that once she started she did not know how she would stop, and with her mother and sister falling into hysterics at the drop of a hat, *someone* had to remain strong.

Taking a deep breath, she ignored the burning in her throat, blinked away the stinging in her eyes, and said, "I appreciate you coming here at such an early hour, Mr. Guthridge. You have been immeasurably helpful."

Gathering up a few wayward papers, the lawyer tucked his satchel under one arm and rubbed his mustache. "I am happy to be of service, Lady Kincaid, especially during this trying time. However, I really do believe your mother—"

"No." Lily tempered the sharp command with her most brilliant smile. "That is to say, I would prefer you kept the clause to yourself… at least for now. Two weeks," she said, confidant she could find a solution in that length of time. "Two weeks and you may tell my mother whatever you wish."

She knew the lawyer didn't like it, but in the end he gave a nod – albeit a reluctant one – and vowed to keep the most unfortunate part of the will to himself for the length of fourteen days.

Lily saw him out, all smiles and bright assurances that everything would be 'quite well', but the moment the door was closed she slumped against it, the last of her strength draining away as she closed her eyes. "Oh Father," she whispered brokenly, "what have you done?"

CHAPTER TWO

CAPTAIN JAMES RIGBY, formerly of the second company in the eighth British battalion, was done fighting. Had been done, if truth be told, for the past two years, but it wasn't until his arm was severed from his body that he was officially declared unfit for duty and sent home to England.

Losing a limb was a funny thing, James reflected as he sat in his study and stared blindly out the window at the darkening sky. He'd watched the doctor cut it off himself, watched him hack away at the rotting flesh and bone with all the finesse of a butcher while he drifted in and out of consciousness. And yet still he was caught by surprise every time he glanced down and saw nothing on the left side of his body save a neatly pinned shirt sleeve.

It had taken three men to hold him down on the table. A fourth to force his jaw open and pour the laudanum down. Even now, five months removed, he could still taste it, just as he could still feel his arm.

He closed his eyes, replaying the bloody memory that still haunted him day and night. A memory he wished he could cut away as easily as the doctor had cut away his flesh and bone.

James' remaining hand curled into a tight fist of frustration that pounded uselessly against the top of his desk, shaking papers and sending a glass figurine toppling over the edge. He waited for the figurine to break. Waited for it to break, as he was broken. Waited for it to shatter, as he was shattered.

But the glass remained intact, and the irony that such a delicate thing could survive a fall unharmed while he, a strong, strapping man of only twenty seven had been reduced to little more than a cripple, did not escape his notice.

He wanted to curse. He wanted to cry. He wanted to shout to the high heavens about how bloody *unfair* it all was, but he knew once he started he might never stop, and so he bottled up the self-pity and the anger and the emotion and buried it in a place so dark it could not help but fade into oblivion.

His heart.

A timid knock sounded at the door, alerting James to who was on the other side even before he heard his sister's soft voice through the thick wood.

"James, are you all right?" she asked hesitantly. "I thought... I thought I heard something."

"Something fell off my desk. Come in, Natty."

The door creaked open a few scant inches and a pale face, oval in shape and quite pretty in design, peeked through.

At seventeen Natalie was a girl on the brink of womanhood, not that James liked to think in such terms although he supposed he would have to start. An arm, he reflected grimly as his once bright, vibrant sister darted nervously into the room, was not the only thing he'd lost during the war.

Time.

The only thing in life that was given and taken in equal measure.

When he went to France five years ago he left behind a rambunctious girl with dirt on her knees and pigtails in her hair. He'd returned to find a somber woman full grown, a woman who knocked where she once would have rushed in. A woman who frowned where she once would have smiled.

They said war changed the men who fought within it, and James knew that to be true. But he also rather thought it changed those left behind as well. The ones forced to wait and worry, never knowing if the next day, the next hour, the next minute would bring good news or bad. The ones forced to carry on with their lives as though nothing were amiss. The ones forced to grow up without a father, a son, a brother…

"I do not want to disturb you," Natalie said, her blue eyes wide and wary.

"You're not." He spoke curtly, adopting the same brusque tone he'd used to send soldiers into battle. A tone that had no place in a gentleman's study. Natalie faltered a step, her lips parting in dismay, and James bit back a growl of frustration. He already garnered enough frightful glances when he walked down the street – he did not need his own sister to fear him as well. And yet fear him she did, if the twist of her hands and the worried look upon her countenance was any indication.

Making a deliberate effort to soften his voice, he nodded towards the leather chair facing his desk and asked if she would like to sit. Natalie did so with great caution, perching on the very edge of the seat as though preparing to flee at a moment's notice.

A silence rose between them like a wall, as unfamiliar as it was uncomfortable, and James could not help but wonder when he'd lost his sister.

Was it the day he left, when she clung to his side and begged through her tears for him not to go? The long months and years that followed? When their father died and she was forced to live with their aunt? Or after he returned, more a monster than a man, with no idea of how to live in polite society?

Frustrated beyond all bearing, James thrust a hand through his hair, pulling the long, unkempt ends taut. He was in desperate need of a haircut, a shave, and, he thought with a sardonic twist of his lips, a new wardrobe with all of the left sleeves removed.

"You look... nice." Belatedly noting Natalie was wearing an ivory ball gown trimmed with light blue lace, James studied her with more attention to detail. Her chestnut brown hair was pulled back from her face and twisted up into one of those bewildering coiffures that defied gravity. Pearls – their mother's, if he was not mistaken – clung to her ears and wrapped around her neck. "Very nice," he said, a frown weighing heavily on his mouth. "What is the occasion?"

For a moment – a moment so quick if he'd blinked he would have missed it – a flash of irritation flickered in Natalie's eyes before she slumped back in her seat, stared up at the ceiling, and mumbled something under her breath.

"Speak up," James demanded, then immediately winced. *You are not on the bloody battlefield taking a report*, he reminded himself sternly. *Calm yourself, man, before you frighten her further*.

"I *said*," Natalie began, her dark eyebrows pulling together, "I knew you would forget."

"Forget?" His frown deepened. "Forget what?"

"The ball at Winswood Estate, hosted by Lord and Lady Heathcliff. It is fine," she said hastily before James could say a word. "I… I did not want to go."

Heathcliff. The name rang a bell of memory deep within the recesses of James' mind. He struggled to recall its origin for a moment, then shrugged and let it go. He would remember in due time. He always did.

Leaning forward onto his remaining arm, James did a sweeping glance of Natalie's attire and said dryly, "Is that why you are wearing a gown fit for a queen?"

Instantly a deep blush took hold of Natalie's cheeks

and her hands passed in a nervous flutter across her lap, smoothing an imaginary wrinkle from the thick folds of her dress. "I told you about the ball over a month ago but I... I suppose you were otherwise occupied."

That was one way to put it. Another – even though he cringed to think of it now – was that he'd been a raging lunatic, drunk off his arse from sunup to sundown, with nary a coherent word spoken (or retained) in between. The pain in his arm had driven him to drink. The fact that the pain came from an arm he no longer had drove him to the brink of lunacy. By sheer will he'd brought himself back from the edge, but the journey had not been an easy one, and James was not so foolish to think it was even halfway finished.

How long would it take, he wondered, until he stopped trying to open a door knob with a hand that no longer existed? How long until the phantom aches eased? How long until he woke in a bed not soaked with his own sweat? How long until he felt a shred of normalcy return?

"I take it the ball is tonight?" he asked after a long pause. The last thing he wanted to do was feel the weight of a dozen stares as he played the part of chaperone, but he supposed there was no getting around it. If he wanted to reacquaint himself into society – which he did, if only for his sister's sake – then there really was no way around it.

Balls were long, tedious affairs filled with intricate dance steps he had never been able to successfully master and idle gossip he had no interest in taking part in. Although now, given his situation, there was *one* upside. No mothers would be sending their sparkly eyed daughters his way to dance, for who in their right mind would want to court the attentions of a cripple? He would be left in peace, Natalie would be able to waltz to her heart's content, and hopefully she would begin to treat him as she used to.

That was all he wanted.

Not an enormous mansion, or a fleet of carriages, or a gorgeous woman on his arm. No, his desires were much simpler than that. All he wanted, all he *needed*, was for life to go back to 'used to'.

"The ball began an hour ago," Natalie whispered, still fussing with her skirts, her eyes downcast and her shoulders rigid.

James stood up. "Then I'd best get changed."

"You… You want to attend?"

Someone – a maid, he assumed – had placed a sprig of holly on the corner of his desk in celebration of the impending holiday. The leaves were a dark, glossy green and felt like wax when he picked up the sprig and twirled it absently between his thumb and forefinger, sending the red berries spinning in circles. "Why don't you ask Mrs. Fieldstone to have the carriage brought round," he said, referring to their head housekeeper, a plump, pleasant woman who had loyally served the Rigby household for three generations. "And I will meet you in the foyer in five minutes."

"Five minutes?" Natalie said doubtfully.

For the first time in recent memory, James' mouth attempted to form a smile. The muscles stretched and tightened, pulling at the sides of his face in a way that was both familiar and forgotten. "Perhaps ten," he said, acknowledging his disheveled appearance with a wry shake of his head.

After sleeping day in and day out on the hard ground, he'd grown accustomed to dirt. Smelling it. Tasting it. Wearing it. To him, the worn out trousers and tunic he was currently wearing were luxurious garments, but in reality they were far more suited for a beggar than a member of the gentry.

He had clothes, of course. More than he knew what to do with. But after being forced to wear a heavy, cumbersome uniform for longer than he cared to remember, James now welcomed comfort over quality. Unfortunately the rest of his peers still favored pomp and circumstance, which meant his current state of dress was a far cry from suitable for a formal ball. In all honesty he could give a flying fig what others thought of him, but he knew his actions and appearance would have a direct effect on Natalie, and so he would try – 'try' being the operative word – to engage in a manner befitting a man of his station.

The Rigby's had never been nobility, but they were gentlemen, their wealth discreetly earned and just as discreetly spent. Their country estate was modest, their townhouse in London rented seasonally, but they had never wanted for money nor suffered due to lack of it.

"How is the marriage mart these days?" James asked as he walked around the side of his desk and out into the hallway. Candles illuminated the narrow passage, sending flickering spheres of light dancing up the walls and over the faces of his ancestors that now existed solely within the confines of silver edged frames. At the end of the hall, James knew, would be his parents, Harold Rigby on one side and Bernice Rigby on the other. Staring endlessly at each other in painted memoriam as they had never stared at each other in life.

James' memories of his mother were vague at best, nonexistent at worst. She'd died of complications shortly after Natalie was born, and their father followed suit eight years later. Still a young, impressionable girl of nine Natalie had gone to live with an aunt while he… he had used his new inheritance to purchase an officer's commission in the army.

"There is no one I am interested in currently." Natalie trailed behind him, quiet as a mouse where she once would have made enough noise to wake the dead. James paused at the end of the hall and turned to face his sister. Even in the flickering shadows she seemed pale and withdrawn; a slim imitation of the laughing, rambunctious girl he remembered.

"What happened to you Natty?" he murmured, drawing on the name he'd used when they were children. His arm ached to wrap around her shoulders, to pull her close and banish the fear he saw in her eyes, but she was already so stiff he feared one touch would be enough to shatter the temporary alliance he'd built between them since his return.

Natalie stared at him, her expression guarded. "Not all wounds can be seen from the outside," she said cryptically.

Something churned inside of James' stomach. It wasn't a pleasant feeling. "Natty, what are you—"

"I will ask to have the carriage brought round and meet you in the foyer," she said, cutting him off mid-sentence before she spun in a swirl of white silk and hurried back down the hall.

Watching her go, James wanted to pound his fist against the wall, his need to strike something tangible so great it was like a living thing clawing at him. *I cannot fight your demons when you won't tell me what they are, Natty*, he thought helplessly. *Not when I have my own to contend with.*

CHAPTER THREE

32 days until Christmas
The Winswood Estate
Home of Sarah & Devlin Heathcliff

THE VERY LAST THING Lily wanted to do was attend a ball, and had it not been hosted by her dearest friend in the entire world she would have skipped it without remorse. Unfortunately, the ball in question *was* being hosted by her dearest friend in the entire world, and thus she found herself dancing at midnight in the arms of a man who possessed both a wandering eye and a heavy instep.

Unable to contain her wince when he trod on her foot for the third – or was it the fourth? – time, Lily bowed out gracefully as the musical strains of the waltz drew to a close. "Thank you for the dance," she said politely even as her attention wandered across the room to where Lady Sarah Heathcliff – best friend and former wallflower extraordinaire – stood beside her tall, dark haired husband, her face tilted up towards his and her doe brown eyes glowing with adoration.

The Viscount of Winswood seemed just as infatuated with his wife as she was with him if the hand resting daringly low on her hip was any indication, and Lily couldn't contain her quiet snort of laughter when his hand slipped lower and was promptly slapped away.

Sarah had married Devlin Heathcliff the winter before after a scandalously short engagement. She'd loved the handsome viscount from afar for years, but had only gotten up the courage to finally make herself known to him after no small amount of urging from Lily. Now, nearly a year into marriage, the two were more in love than ever before and Lily took her fair share of credit for their blissful happily-ever-after.

If only finding a husband of her own could be so easy.

As she retreated to the refreshment table and helped herself to a handful of grapes, Lily could not help but scowl. Nearly every eligible bachelor in existence was in attendance tonight, but nary a one had managed to catch her eye.

They were either too young or too old. Too arrogant or too meek. Too talkative or too quiet. Too... well, too *everything*. She wasn't looking for perfection. Truly she wasn't. But surely there had to something better out there than the current crop of fop minded gentleman who wouldn't know an intelligent conversation if it smacked them upside their hideous wigs.

The very idea that she would most likely have to pick someone from this very room to marry was so depressing she set her plate of grapes aside without eating a single one.

"Are they too sour?"

In hindsight it was a very good thing Lily *had* put down the grapes, for if she was still holding them they would have certainly flown every which way. "My goodness," she said with a laugh as she spun around.

The girl who had snuck up behind her was young, no more than sixteen or seventeen if Lily had to hazard a guess, with chestnut colored hair that framed a delicate, heart shaped face, sweeping eyebrows and pale, serious eyes. "You certainly startled me," she continued with a bright, cheerful smile intended to put the visibly nervous girl at ease. "No, the grapes are not sour. Well, perhaps they are, but I wouldn't know. I did not eat any. It seems I do not have much of an appetite this evening."

The girl glanced down at her shoes peeking out from beneath the hem of her ivory gown. "Neither do I," she whispered.

"Then why are you by the refreshment table?"

"Hiding," the girl said succinctly, peeking up through her lashes.

She certainly was a pretty thing, Lily mused. Much too pretty to be skulking around in the corner of the room. Her shy, quiet demeanor reminded Lily of her own sister Elsa, a mouse like girl who was as different from Lily as the sun was from the moon.

Lily had urged Elsa to attend tonight but she had remained at home with their mother, leaving Lily no choice but to come with Aunt Fontaine as her chaperone, a dear woman in her mid-sixties who was half deaf and very fond of naps.

No doubt she was off dozing in a corner at this very moment, for Lily hadn't seen her in nearly an hour which was plenty of time for Aunt Fontaine to find a comfortable chair, arrange her fan so it *appeared* she was watching all of the dancing, and fall promptly asleep.

"In hiding?" Lily echoed. "You really shouldn't be, you know. Not when you look so stunning. Why, I remember my first few balls. I was an absolute mess! Hair every which way and you don't even want to *know* what my dresses looked like."

"I highly doubt that," the girl said dubiously.

Lily grinned and perched a hand on her hip. "Trust me. It took quite a while until I hit my stride. At least your come out is during the Little Season. You will have plenty of time to practice before London."

Taking place in the country as opposed to the city, the *ton's* Little Season ran during the holidays while parliament was on respite and the upper class needed something to occupy their time. It was a more subdued affair than its counterpart, but there were still balls and luncheons aplenty. Sarah and Devlin's little soiree was but the first of a half dozen or so balls leading up to Christmas... and Lily's deadline.

Suddenly her smile became more forced, and it fell from her face all together when the girl asked, "Are you married, then?"

"No... I am not." The words tasted bitter on her tongue and she forced them out with difficulty. How easy that question used to be for her to answer! No, I am not married. No, I do not plan on marrying in the near future. Why not? Well, quite simply because I want to marry for love.

Marry for love... A luxury she could no longer afford.

Again Lily wondered why her father would do such a

thing to her, and again she could not fathom a reason. He had loved her. She knew he had. But just as importantly he had *understood* her. He knew she was not one of those women who dreamed day in and day out of finding the perfect husband, having the perfect wedding, and raising the perfect children. She wanted more for her life. She wanted more for *herself.* She wanted to travel to all the places she'd read about in her father's atlases and experience new cultures and learn new languages. She wanted to live to the fullest with no regrets, and die an old woman content in her bed knowing she had done everything she set out to do. She did *not* want to marry a man she barely knew and spend the rest of her days chasing children and making certain the good silver was set out for their dinner guests.

And yet what choice did she have? She could not allow everything her mother owned to be passed on to Cousin Eustace. Even if he wasn't an insufferable old goat with a nasty streak, Lily could not countenance the idea of her sweet mother being forced to ask for every shilling and pence as though she were some lowly beggar instead of the lovely, gracious lady she was. Not to mention how it would affect Elsa's debut in the spring, or their entire future.

Lily had seen firsthand what happened when a family's inheritance was passed on to a distant relative. The very same had happened to one of her friends from finishing school. The girl's father died, leaving the fate of his wife and three daughters (not to mention his fortune) in the hands of his brother. For a while all was well, but within the year the brother married, had a child of his own, and gradually began to take more and more of the inheritance that should have been saved for his sister-in-law and nieces.

Since the law so heavily favored men over women there was nothing that could be done. The last Lily heard of her friend she was living with her mother and sisters in a small two bedroom townhouse and was looking for employment as a governess.

I shall not let the same thing happen to Elsa, Lily vowed silently. *Come hell or high water, I will find a husband.*

She needed someone handsome, but not in the pretty way she detested. Someone kind, but not overly sweet. Someone intelligent, but not boring. Someone... Well, someone exactly like *him*.

As her gaze scoured the crowded room, Lily found her attention inexplicably drawn as though by some invisible force to the far opposite corner where a tall, dark haired man stood slouched against a large potted fern. Staring at him, she felt the queerest of flutters in her belly and a flush the likes of which she rarely experienced bloomed across her exposed collarbone.

She did not know what drew her eye to the man. Except for his height, there was nothing of note about him. He was not dressed in the best of clothes, nor the worst. His hair, pulled back in a sleek tail, was neither the shortest nor the longest. His face, with its sharply drawn cheekbones and prominent nose, was a few rugged lines away from handsome. His mouth, slanted at one side in an unmistakable show of disdain, hovered two notches above cruel.

No, he was no one of note. But in one long, lingering glance Lily found herself utterly and irrevocably captivated.

"Do you know who that is?" she whispered, slanting a sideways glance at her silent companion who she had, in all honesty, forgotten about until this very moment. Not that it was her fault. The girl – whoever she was – made about as much of an impact as the wallpaper, and heavens knew the brown and white pattern was dreadfully dull.

"Who is who?" the girl asked, blinking her large eyes

and reminding Lily very much of a tiny barn owl.

"That man standing in the corner over there by the plant." In her usual brash style, Lily lifted one hand and pointed straight at the stranger who had managed to capture her undivided attention. "He is dressed all in black. Do you know his name?"

For some reason the question caused the girl's cheeks to fill with color and her fingers to interlace so tightly her knuckles gleamed white in the candlelight. "I... I..."

"Well? Who is he?" Patience had never been one of Lily's virtues. She was of half a mind to march across the floor and speak to the stranger herself, but with the faintest of tremors in her voice the girl finally answered.

"His name is Captain James Rigby," she said with obvious reluctance, "and he is my brother."

CHAPTER FOUR

JAMES COULD *FEEL* the woman's eyes on him. He willed her to look away but she persisted until he finally lifted his head and met her stare for bold, unwavering stare across the crowded ballroom.

She was stunningly beautiful, of course. Flawless ivory skin. Ebony hair coiled in an intricate twist at the nape of her neck. A navy blue dress so dark it could have been black if not for the shimmers of color revealed when she shifted her weight to the side. The gown fit her like a glove, tight around her breasts and nipped in waist before spilling out in a wave of soft fabric. Her features were delicate, from the curve of her cupids bow mouth to the slight tilt of her nose. And her eyes… James sucked in a breath. Even from this distance he would see her eyes were the loveliest violet he'd ever beheld.

"Fairy," he murmured, knowing no one could hear him, not caring if they did. From the very moment he arrived he'd sequestered himself in a lonesome corner of the room, preferring the company of plants to people. He had planned on giving Natalie another hour at most – the poor girl wasn't even dancing – before he made their excuses. He didn't belong here. Not anymore.

Oh, once he had. Once he would have strolled across the room, taken the violet eyed beauty by the hand, and swept her into a waltz. Once he would have drawn her outside and seduced a kiss from those perfect lips under the silvery glow of the moonlight. Once he would have left her wanting as *he* was now left wanting.

Wanting for courage.

Wanting for normalcy.

Wanting for his bloody arm back.

His teeth clenched as the all too familiar throbbing in a body part that no longer existed began to plague him. One more hour be damned. He and Natalie were leaving now, whether she liked it or not.

Tearing his gaze away from the fairy he searched the room with the same hard eyed meticulousness he had used to search for bodies on the battlefield. When one circuit revealed nothing he straightened and took a step forward, his muscles coiling and tensing beneath the heavy wool of his jacket. By sheer happenstance he glanced at the violet eyed woman again... and this time saw Natalie standing beside her, her face pale and her

143

hands clenched tight.

James did not charge through the crowd, but he might as well have. He walked with long legged purpose, his gaze never leaving the frightened countenance of his sister, not acknowledging the men and women who scrambled to clear his path with little squeaks of alarm.

"What is it?" he said roughly once he'd reached her. Ignoring the woman at her side entirely, he lifted his hand to touch Natalie's shoulder, but jerked it back when she flinched and cowered. "Natalie, I…" Jaw clenching furiously, he turned to the side. "You do not have to be afraid of me."

"Not afraid of you?" the fairy chirped. "After the way you came marching over here? Why, I would be positively terrified. Mayhap you should try it again. You are in a ballroom, Captain Rigby, not a battlefield."

James spun around, disbelief widening his eyes and thinning his mouth. Of all the nerve… "I do not recall asking your opinion," he growled.

The fairy batted her eyelashes – her incredibly long, incredibly dark eyelashes – at him. "What a coincidence, as I do not recall asking your permission. Lady Lily Kincaid," she said, extending one slender hand enclosed in a satin glove. "I only tell you that because you seem to

144

be at a disadvantage, as I knew your name before you came stomping over here. Please, no need to thank me." Her lips quirked in a manner that irritated even as it aroused. "I can see social etiquette is difficult for you and I wouldn't want you to strain yourself."

James stared hard at her hand, but did not take it and after a moment Lily shrugged and let her arm drop. "What are you doing with my sister?"

Her lashes fluttered again, causing a long, low pull in James' gut that he resolutely ignored. "Isn't it obvious? I am making friends with your poor sister to get to you. That is what you are thinking, is it not?" She snorted and, to his disbelief, rolled her eyes. At *him*. When was the last time anyone, let alone a delicate slip of a woman who barely came up to his chin, had the audacity to show such disrespect? His brow furrowed. In all honesty, he couldn't remember.

"That's what all you tall, brooding types think," Lily continued, nonplussed by his dark glower. "Your sister and I were having an absolutely fine conversation before you muddled into it, thank you very much, and we shall continue to do so after you've muddled your way back out."

James' mouth opened. Closed. Opened again.

"Natalie, come with me."

"Natalie, stay right where you are."

The woman, James decided instantly, was no fairy. No, she was far too obnoxious for that. A sprite, he thought with annoyance. The kind that were fabled to cause all sorts of mischief and mayhem. "May I speak with you in private?" he bit out.

Lily arched one dark eyebrow. "Certainly."

He went to reach for her… with his left arm. The motion was so ingrained he forgot that part of his body no longer existed until it was too late. Thrown off balance by his own momentum he staggered to the side, bumping hard into the refreshment table. Pastries wobbled and grapes spilled out across the floor as he righted himself and, without a backwards glance, stalked to the nearest door and yanked it open.

The door led to a narrow hallway, the hallway to a dimly lit parlor.

Flames slumbered in the fireplace. James brought them to life with a few sharp jabs of a metal poker before throwing his body down into a leather chair and staring into the newly aroused flickers of orange and yellow light with an intensity that made his head ache.

When the door creaked open he didn't turn around. He

didn't need to. There was only one person fool enough to chase after a man who was so clearly unfit for social company, and he had no intention of talking to her.

"Go away," he said flatly.

The quiet shuffle of slippers on wood, a whisper of crinoline, and a short, annoyed exhalation of breath announced Lily's arrival. "You said you wanted to speak to me in private."

"I changed my mind."

"Well, that may be, but since I am already here you might as well say what you wanted to say."

James' growl was nothing short of animalistic in nature. He curled his hand into the armrest, digging his fingers into the buttery soft leather, using it as an anchor to hold him to chair. "Leave. Me. Alone."

Lily sighed. "I know we have only just met, but I must admit I feel—"

"I do not care," James interrupted through gritted teeth, "what you bloody well *feel*. All I care is that you GET THE HELL OUT!"

Absolute silence followed his outburst.

James' throat convulsed as he attempted to swallow the shame that accompanied losing his temper in such a vile way. To yell at a stranger for virtually no reason was bad enough, but to yell at a gently bred *lady*... Disgraceful. Beneath his tightly wound cravat his chest burned red and he buried his face in the crook of his shoulder while he waited for the inevitable tears to start and the door to slam.

Only there *were* no tears or slamming of doors, and after what felt like a small eternity curiosity finally forced James to turn in his chair.

"Yes, I am still here," Lily remarked mildly. Standing in the middle of the shadowy room with her hands perched high on her hips, she stared down her nose at him and sniffed. "As you can see, I have not collapsed in a fit of hysterics nor have I rushed from the room crying for my mother. I am afraid it will take more than a bit of shouting to frighten me off, Captain Rigby. At the very least more cursing. You are quite loud, but not terribly inventive. Should I give you some better words to use the next time you feel like letting off a bit of steam?" Her lips curved. "I admit I know quite a few."

"Who *are* you?" he asked in genuine bewilderment.

She stepped forward, moving so gracefully it seemed as though she wasn't moving at all, except one moment she was across the room and the next she was leaning against the back of his chair, her face so close to his he could see a star shaped freckle high on her left cheek. The urge to kiss that delightful little freckle, to see if her ivory skin felt as soft as it looked, to know what she tasted like against his mouth, was so overwhelming James abruptly spun around and shoved himself forward, resting on the very edge of the chair, as far from Lily as he could possibly get without standing.

"My name is Lily Kincaid, as I have told you" she said quietly. "Although I believe the better question to ask would be who *you* are, Captain Rigby."

He glared into the flames. "My sister told you who I am."

"You name, perhaps, and your rank, but those two things do not tell me who you truly are. I would think you were still a soldier, for you hold yourself like one, but you do not wear the uniform. You possess the arrogance of a lord, but not the patience for the mindless social games that accompany such a title. A gentleman would describe you best, perhaps, except I fear there is nothing gentle about you." Lily lowered her voice, lowered her head, and whispered into his ear, "So who are you, Captain James Rigby?"

She smelled, James thought with an irrational surge of anger, *like peaches*. How the bloody hell could she smell like peaches in the middle of winter? The sweet, tart scent reminded him of a childhood long ago spent visiting a now dead aunt and uncle in the small coastal town of Brest. They'd owned a modest estate, and on the estate there was a poorly tended orchard of peach trees. He and Natalie had spent many an afternoon playing hide-and-seek in the secluded grove, eating fruit until their bellies ached and their chins were stained yellow from the sweet nectar of the peaches.

How simple life had been back then... And how very much he did not want to remember, nor be reminded, of innocence lost and never regained.

"Who are you to ask such a question?" Unable to remain still any longer, he lurched clumsily to his feet and turned so he felt the heat of the fire on his back, careful to keep the leather chair as a barrier between them. He had been too long without a woman to trust himself... especially around one as beautiful – and infuriating – as Lily Kincaid.

"No one in particular." Lily trailed her fingertips along the top of the chair, caressing the soft leather. James imagined what it would feel like to feel those fingers trailing along his own skin... and felt himself go hard. "I am just a woman," she continued, oblivious to the physical effect she had on him, "who saw a man across a ballroom and thought 'now *that* is someone worth knowing'."

"I am no one," he said gruffly. *Least of all someone fit for the likes of you*, he added silently.

Even if he wasn't a cripple, even if he could make it through the day without drinking half a bottle of whisky, even if he didn't wake up every night soaked in his own sweat screaming out the names of men who were long buried in the ground, he wouldn't have been a match for a lady like Lily. She was too delicate. Too easily broken. Too... too everything right, where he was everything wrong. No doubt someone had put the idea in her head that it would be a passing amusement to indulge in a bit of heavy flirting with an officer, and pure happenstance had brought her to him.

At the thought, James' eyes narrowed and his mouth hardened. He was no toy to be picked up, admired, and cast aside at the whim of some bored debutante. Perhaps it was time for Lily to learn if you played with fire, you ran the risk of getting burned.

His mind made up to teach her a lesson – he *had* warned her to leave, after all – James stalked around the side of the chair and stopped short in front of her. The firelight bathed them in its glow, casting flickering shadows that climbed the walls in long, sinuous strokes of black edged with orange and red. Beyond the study faint strains of music could be heard, a reminder of a ball James had already forgotten about. His thoughts veered to Natalie and obligations better served elsewhere, but then Lily wet her bottom lip with a tiny flick of her tongue and he couldn't think at all.

She tipped her head back, her unusually colored eyes steady on his. The air itself seemed to hum, filled with an electricity so potent it set the hairs at the nape of his neck on edge. His hand clenched, muscles tightening and bulging beneath his overcoat. One step closer. Another. The lapels of his jacket brushed against the bodice of her gown. Lily drew in a sharp breath. Her eyes closed…

Without warning his determination wavered.

Like a ship whose rudder had been knocked askew James was thrown off course and left reeling in waves of self-doubt and indecision. What woman in her right mind would want to kiss him? What woman would want to be held by a man who was less than whole? *None*, came the immediate answer, *and certainly not this one. She's too good for you, James. You're a crippled ex-soldier who is most likely more than a little half mad. Leave before you're the one left, you bloody fool.*

Lily's eyes opened. "Captain Rigby? What is the matter?"

"I… I…" But words failed him and, without knowing what else to do, he shoved roughly past and fled the room as though the very demons of hell were nipping at his heels.

CHAPTER FIVE

WELL THAT HAD certainly not gone as planned.

As she watched the door to the study swing back and forth, propelled into motion by James' hasty exit, Lily made a soft humming sound of distress and sank into the nearest chair. All she wanted was a bit of conversation, and – if she were being honest – a kiss. The notion of James' mouth covering her own had been a thrilling one, and it had taken all of her self-control not to launch herself at him while she waited impatiently for him to go about the business of putting his lips on hers.

Never one to shy away from passion, Lily had indulged in her fair share of kisses since coming of age, although she'd minded her manners and never gone any further than allowing the occasional hand to cup her breast in the dark shadows of a garden. She was willing to do more, but it would have to be with the right man.

Was Captain James Rigby that man? It was too soon to tell.

The initial spark of attraction she so desperately craved and so rarely received was there, which was most definitely a promising sign. Lily could count on one hand the number of men who had managed to turn her head since her debut and there was no denying she'd felt drawn to James the moment she spied him across the room.

It was rather unfortunate he possessed such a churlish temperament, but she supposed if she had suffered through the horrors of war and lost an arm in the process she would be rather churlish as well. It was what lurked *beneath* the rough exterior that truly interested her.

He was someone who had experienced the world. Who had lived outside the four corners of London and seen the gritty, raw side of life never witnessed by lords of the manor living safely within the confines of their estates sipping port and discussing the weather.

The door creaked open, washing light into the dark study. Lily looked up expectantly, her heart beginning to pound as she anticipated James' return, but the tiny jolt of excitement subsided with a faint flutter of disappointment when she saw it was her dear friend Sarah, not the enigmatic captain, who had come looking for her.

"Lily? Is that you?" Squinting into the study, Sarah pushed the door open wider and took two hesitant steps inside. Dressed in a stunning plum colored gown with her golden hair twisted into a demure coiffure, she managed to look equal parts bookish and beautiful. Always the shyer and more demure of the two, Sarah had finally found her inner confidence after marrying Devlin, and Lily had never known her friend to be happier.

"Yes," she answered with a sigh, "you have found me."

"What in heaven's name are you doing sitting by yourself in the dark?" Her skirts swishing against her ankles, Sarah moved briskly across the room and lit two beeswax candles before sinking into a chaise lounge opposite of Lily's chair with a little *oof* of breath. "I am quite tired," she admitted. "Devlin has insisted on dancing nearly every waltz, even though I told him having one's husband fill up their card is not at all *de rigueur*."

"And you would not have it any other way," Lily said with a grin.

Sarah's cheeks brightened ever so slightly. "No, I suppose not. But enough about me." She waved her hand in the air, causing the firelight to reflect off her gold wedding band. "Has something happened? Why are you in hiding?" A line appeared between her pale eyebrows as she frowned. "Was someone untoward? If they were, tell me their name and I will have Devlin—"

"No, no, nothing has happened. Even if it had, do you really think I would be sulking in a room by myself?" *Even though that is exactly what I am doing*, she thought silently. *Sulking because, for once in my life, a man did not go out of his way to please me.*

Lily had never put much stock in physical appearance, but she was an intelligent woman, and she knew her beauty was held in high regard. As a result men had been courting her favor since she was a girl of fourteen, which explained all the kisses. It did *not* explain why James had left her in the lurch, choosing to brave the crowded ballroom – something he clearly despised – rather than kiss her. Her nose wrinkling as she recalled his expression of disgust, she shifted her right shoulder back and gave a discreet sniff. Well, she didn't smell. At least she had that in her favor, if not much else where the ex-soldier was concerned.

"Lily, dear…"

"Yes?"

"What are you doing?"

Lily let her shoulder drop and crossed her slender legs at the ankle beneath the voluminous folds of her gown. "Seeing if I stink."

Sarah released a startled laugh. "Why would you stink?"

"I do not know." Lily shrugged. "I just thought that I might and so I was checking to see if I did, but I don't. At least I don't think I do. Then again, perhaps one cannot smell oneself. You should do it."

But Sarah, her expression wary, was already shaking her head. "Do what? *Smell* you? Lily, are you certain nothing is amiss? You are acting very strangely." Her countenance abruptly softening, she reached between their chairs to squeeze Lily's hand. "I know you must still be mourning your father. I rather thought attending a ball this early might be too much, but you always seem to do best when you are the busiest. Do you want me to have a carriage brought round to take you home?"

"A carriage is the last thing I need," Lily said cryptically.

"Well, if you don't want a carriage, what is it you *do* want?"

"A husband," Lily said after a long pause. Gently

extricating her hand from Sarah's grasp she sat back, crossed her arms over her chest, and looked directly at her friend. "I want a husband."

NATALIE WATCHED HER brother storm back into ballroom from the safety of the refreshment table. Wedged between plates of desserts and an oversized potted fern she was able to remain silently in the background, a true wallflower if ever there was one.

It wasn't that she did not *want* attention. In truth, she was starving for it. Unfortunately, it was when she received attention, especially of the male variety, that the problems began. Problems that had turned into symptoms of an illness she feared was ruining her life. An illness she knew the cause of, but not the cure.

Shortness of breath.

Perspiration on her palms.

An embarrassing stutter.

A deep, cloying fear that suffocated from the inside out.

She hated that James triggered the illness. Hated that she was afraid of her own brother. Hated the wounded look that flashed across his face whenever she flinched away. He had returned from the battlefield needing help, and all she had to give was hurt.

But how could she ever explain the source of her fear? At the mere thought Natalie's eyes pinched shut and her heart rate sped up. An icy chill raced down her spine, extending all the way to the balls of her feet and out to the tips of her fingers. If she told he would know, and if he knew… With a soft cry she curled her hand into a fist and pressed it hard against her mouth to contain the sickness that threatened to spill up and out. If he knew, it would begin all over again.

Needing to distract herself from thoughts best left buried, Natalie opened her eyes and scanned the crowded room for James. Amidst the laughing faces his stern, unsmiling countenance was easy to spot. He was already looking at her, and when their gazes met his head tilted to the side, his eyes flicking towards the couples who were dancing in silent question.

"*No,*" Natalie mouthed, suppressing a tremble. It was all she could do to stand in the same room with so many men and not scream bloody murder. To actually dance with one… To allow his hands to touch her body… Again the wave of sickness swelled within her breast, and again she managed to fight it back. No. No, she would not be dancing tonight, nor any other night, not if she could help it.

She hoped if she attended the ball tonight things would be different. That *she* would be different, but now she knew there was to be no easy fix for her illness.

James returned to his corner. Natalie remained in hers.

What a pair they made, their current situation made all the worse by the fact that they hadn't always been so miserable. Once they'd been happy, blissfully so, living in a world beyond war and nightmares and hot, breathy voices asking if you wanted a tickle before bedtime. Now their world was fractured, their happiness only a memory.

What Natalie wouldn't give to have things go back to the way they were. If not for her, then for James. He'd sacrificed so much. The life he knew. The family he loved. The future that would have been his if he hadn't given it all up to go fight for queen and country.

She wished she could be the one to bring him back from the brink of darkness, but she feared her own despair was so great she would only serve to tip them both over the edge. He needed someone stronger than she to show him the light. To show him how to live and laugh and love again.

He had friends who wanted to help, but the ones who went to war with him had not returned and those who

161

remained did not understand.

No, he needed someone else. Someone who had not known him before. Someone who would not mind having their feelings hurt. Someone strong enough to ease his pain, but gentle enough to soothe his fear. Someone loud enough to drown out his past. Someone bright enough to help draw him into a future free from worry and regret.

Someone, Natalie thought as a sudden idea took root, *exactly like Lily Kincaid.*

Closing her eyes, she drew on what little faith she had left and wished for a miracle.

CHAPTER SIX

29 days until Christmas

"WE ARE RUINED. Absolutely, positively ruined." Clasping a hand to her forehead, Regina Kincaid staggered dramatically across the room and flung herself onto a chaise lounge. Reclining until she was flat on her back, she closed her eyes and moaned loudly. "Please have one of the maids fetch me a cooling cloth, Elsa. I fear a terrible headache coming on."

Lily's sigh was long and suffering. "Elsa, remain where you are," she said, directing her sister a narrow eyed glare that had the younger girl hastily returning to her chair. "Mother, you are not ill. It is your imagination."

"It is not," Regina insisted even as she sat up on her elbow and opened her eyes. "I really do not feel well. A fever," she said decisively. "I am most definitely coming down with a fever."

"And furthermore, we are *not* ruined," Lily continued as if her mother had not spoken a word. "I will take care of everything. I promise."

The weight of that promise weighed heavily on her shoulders, but she kept her back straight and her chin up. She even managed a smile, although it was more for Elsa's benefit than her own for the poor dear looked absolutely terrified. Crouching in front of her sister, she took both of Elsa's hands in hers and squeezed tight. "Look at me," she said firmly. Elsa lifted her head, her blue eyes clearly troubled. "Nothing will happen to us, do you understand?"

"But Cousin Eustace said—"

"Cousin Eustace is a pig." *And that is a compliment compared to what I truly think of him*, Lily added silently.

Yesterday evening Eustace and his wife Venetia, a stick like woman with dark squinty eyes and a penchant for cruel gossip, had joined them for dinner. Eustace made quick work of revealing the will to Regina, who had – as expected – taken the news quite poorly. It took all the self-control Lily possessed not to kick out the cousins on the spot, and she'd spent the rest of dinner plotting the most creative ways to throttle Eustace and his smirking wife.

All through the night in the bedroom across from hers she had heard her mother tossing and turning. This morning Regina wasted no time in calling a family meeting in the library – the only room below stairs boasting a fireplace – and it was clear the contents of the will were weighing heavily on her mind.

Lily hated seeing Regina and Elsa so worried. They were both sweet, gentle souls who looked to others to care for them, and now they were looking to her. Self-doubt nagged at her like a sore tooth, the source of the discomfort vague and relentless. What if she *couldn't* find someone to marry before Christmas? What if everything they owned really *did* go to Cousin Eustace and the terrible Venetia? What if this was one problem she could not solve?

"Lily?" Elsa's timid voice cut through Lily's dark thoughts like a beacon of light.

"Yes darling, what is it?"

"I am frightened," her sister confessed.

"Frightened?" Giving Elsa's hands one last squeeze, Lily bounded to her feet and feigned her brightest smile yet. "Frightened of what, dearest?"

"Of what will happen to us."

"Nothing will happen," Lily said firmly. "Isn't that

right, Mother?"

Regina may have been a woman of small courage, but she'd always stood strong where her daughters were concerned. "You know your sister always has an answer for everything, just like her father. We will be fine and you are not to worry." Sitting up, Regina shook her finger at her youngest daughter. "You know when you worry you frown, and frowning is how wrinkles grow."

"Oh for heaven's sake," Lily muttered. "Mother, Elsa does not have wrinkles. She is sixteen years of age!"

"She doesn't have wrinkles *yet*," Regina said with a sniff, "but she will if she keeps frowning! Why, Lady Hatfield's daughter is only fourteen and the poor dear already has crow marks! It is because she laughs too much. Giggling all the time, that one. Never a sober thought in her head."

Elsa's fingers drifted to her face. "Do *I* have crow marks?" she asked worriedly.

"Let me get my magnifying glass and see."

Regina sprang out of the chaise lounge with surprising zest given she had been on death's door but a few moments ago, and Lily stepped neatly to the side, never one to get in her mother's way when she was on a mission. She wanted to shake them both for being so ridiculous, but she knew it was better for Regina and Elsa to worry about make believe lines and wrinkles than the real problem at hand.

"I am taking Mr. Betram for a walk," she announced when Regina returned from the parlor with an oversized magnifying glass and promptly held it up to Elsa's face.

"A walk?" Regina said without looking up. "Lily dear, it is snowing out. You know Mr. Betram doesn't like the snow."

Lily glanced out the window and saw that it was, indeed, snowing. White flakes spiraled lazily down from an overcast sky, slowly covering the frost tipped grass in a shifting blanket of white. "I will not take him very far. Just to the end of the lane and back. It's good for him to stretch his legs."

Mr. Betram, so named because he bore a striking resemblance to their dressmaker's husband, was the Kincaid's family dog. A short, squat beagle with sorrowful brown eyes and a permanently puzzled expression, he lived in the barn behind the house and took his job of guarding the old, dilapidated structure quite seriously even though he was half blind and more than likely fully deaf. Time and again Lily and her father had tried to coax him to stay inside the house, but within an hour or so he always began to howl and scratch at the door, two sounds Regina could not abide.

"You should not go by yourself. Take Aunt Fontaine with you. It will be good for her to move about as well. Oh, Elsa, I believe I have found a wrinkle!"

Over her sister's distressed squeals Lily said, "Aunt Fontaine is still fast asleep and likely to remain so until afternoon tea. I will not be gone for more than an hour." She paused in the doorway, waiting for her mother to object, but Regina's mind was on other matters and she waved her eldest daughter on with an absent flick of her wrist.

Bundling herself up in a fur lined cloak, dark red scarf, and matching mittens Lily tuck her curls to one side, drew the hood up over her head, and hurried outside before her mother came to her senses and realized she was leaving the house without a proper chaperone.

She walked briskly between the snowflakes, following a narrow footpath that led around the side of the house and meandered down to the barn. The metal latch was frozen shut, but after a few strategic kicks of her boot the door slid sideways with a groan. She found Mr. Betram curled up in a pile of straw, his deep, even breaths indicating he was fast asleep. A stray cat, its white fur sticking out in tufts, watched her with lofty regard from atop a bucket.

"Good morning," Lily said politely.

The cat meowed, stretched, and leapt down to twist around her legs, butting her with its tiny head.

"Are you Mr. Betram's new friend, then? We shall have to come up with a name for you, and some food as well. I imagine the mice are fairly scarce this time of year. I sincerely hope you do not have fleas," she said, her nose wrinkling. The cat tilted its head to the side and meowed again, louder this time. Lily bit back a smile. "You are right. That was quite rude of me. Well, if you don't mind, I need to borrow Mr. Betram. I shall return him safe and sound, I promise."

The cat returned to its bucket and Lily gently woke up the beagle. He rolled to his feet with a snort and a snuffle, blinking the sleep from his big brown eyes, and when he saw who had come to visit his tail began to wag with such enthusiasm he knocked the cat's bucket aside and sent the smaller animal dashing into the shadows.

"Now you've done it," Lily said as she righted the bucket before tying a long piece of rope to Mr. Betram's leather collar. Even half blind and deaf the beagle was prone to wandering, and Lily's greatest fear was that he would run off after a rabbit and never be able to find his way home again. Kneeling, she gave him a quick hug, laughed when he licked her face, and led him out into the snow. "Come on, then. Just a quick walk and then you can go back to sleep."

The beagle toddled along obediently, pausing every now and then to sniff and scratch at the frozen ground, but a gentle tug was enough to get him moving again.

They walked side by side down the middle of the long, twisting lane that led to the main road. The snow that had fallen thus far was undisturbed, smooth and white as a fresh piece of parchment. Smoke curled cheerfully from the chimneys of the houses they passed, but the windows were dim and nothing stirred save Lily, Mr. Betram, and four black crows that clacked and cawed high up in the trees. No doubt everyone was still tucked cozily in their beds, which is where Lily would have been had her mother not woken the entire household at the crack of dawn with her fretful pacing.

Her mouth twisting, Lily stepped off the side of the lane to let Mr. Betram sniff at a tree trunk while she mulled over her options.

There was no question time was running out. Wreaths swathed in red ribbon and decorative candles beaming from nearly every window were constant reminders that Christmas was only a few short weeks away. She needed to find a husband, and soon.

When the will was first read Lily had been arrogant enough to assume she would be able to find the perfect man before her father's deadline. That idea had quickly gone by the wayside following Sarah and Devlin's ball, where she quickly discovered there *were* no perfect men. At least none where she was concerned. The only one who had come too close to sparking her interest was Captain James Rigby, but the damn man had run away rather than kiss her, and even though she'd looked high and low there had been no sign of him for the remainder of the ball.

"Impossible," she muttered under her breath, kicking hard at a lump of snow. Unfortunately the lump turned out to be a rock, and Lily cried out in pain when her toes collided with the unyielding object. Even more unfortunately it was at that precise moment that Mr. Betram miraculously spotted a fox across the field, and when he yanked against his rope in an effort to give chase Lily was so focused on her bruised foot she forgot to hold tight.

With one deep, resounding bay he was off, belly

crawling under an old, decrepit wooden fence and bursting out the other side with such enthusiasm he tripped over his own paws and rolled twice, coating his wiggling body in snow before he scrambled to his feet and headed pell-mell for the other side of the field as fast as his short little legs would carry him.

"Mr. Betram, NO!" Hobbling forward, Lily wrapped her hands around the top rail of the fence and yelled for her beloved beagle until her voice was hoarse, but it was to no avail. Mr. Betram was gone.

JAMES WAS OUT for a peaceful morning ride, hoping to clear his head of the demented thoughts that perverted it during the night, when a woman's alarmed shrieks sliced through the air, spurring him into action.

He chased the noise to its source, not knowing what he would find, but automatically fearing the worst. An overturned carriage with bodies scattered in the snow, their limbs twisted at grotesque angles. A highway robber with a dagger pressed up against a man's throat while his wife screamed and pleaded, her face ashen as the snow. A young child floating face down in the icy water of a pond while his mother cried in anguish from the shore. Scenario after gruesome scenario flashed through his mind as he cantered down the lane, each one more horrible than the last.

Instead, he found Lily: clutching a fence, hopping on one foot like a deranged lunatic, screaming another man's name.

He shouldn't have known it was her. She wore a heavy cloak, the fur lined hood pulled up and over her hair. Her face was turned away, her brilliant amethyst eyes hidden from view. Still he knew, beyond a shadow of a doubt, that the same woman who had turned him inside out at the ball was standing before him now.

No, not standing.

Hopping.

"Might I ask what you are doing?" He dismounted in an awkward shuffle of legs and limb – following the amputation his doctor warned he should never sit astride a horse again; James had told the man to go to hell – and led his mount to the side of the road.

Lily startled at the sound of his voice and whirled around, causing the hood of her cloak to fall back and her hair to spill out in a wave of dark silk. Her eyes narrowed, then widened with recognition. "Good morning, Captain Rigby."

James had the sudden, foolish urge to tip his hat, but

he kept his hand wrapped tight around his horse's reins and nodded his head instead. "Lady Kincaid."

"Out for an early ride?" she inquired politely, as though she hadn't just been yelling at the top of her lungs into an empty field.

James blinked. *The woman*, he decided, *was mad as a hatter.* "I am."

"Excellent. I fear people spend far too much time indoors during the winter which, as I am sure you know, is bad for the constitution. At least I think so. What do you think, Captain Rigby?"

He thought she looked beautiful standing in the snow with her hair a tangle of curls around her shoulders and her cheeks flushed from the cold. He thought she was, without any sense of exaggeration, the most stunning woman he'd ever seen. And he thought he wanted to push her up against the fence, cup her lovely face in the hard palm of his hand, and ravish her mouth until they were both senseless and gasping for breath. "I…" He paused, cleared his throat, and tried again. "I agree." Even though by now he had no idea what the hell he was agreeing to.

Lily smiled, although a slight line between her brows indicated her distress. "I was taking Mr. Betram for a walk, but then he saw a fox and I forgot to hold tight and

174

now he has run off," she explained, although of course for James it was no explanation at all.

Beside him his horse snorted and rubbed the length of his face against James' thick wool jacket. He returned the show of affection in kind, absently rubbing behind the bay's ear in a spot he knew the older gelding liked scratched, and the horse blew smoky plumes of air through his oversized nostrils, warming the side of James' neck.

"Your horse likes you," Lily said. She sounded surprised.

"We like each other," James acknowledged. "I have owned him since he was a two year old colt." Gangly and untrained, the bay had been a gift from his father. The gelding – named Biscuit for his brown coat – was nearing his twentieth year. He did not possess the energy he'd once had as a youngster, but his spirit was unchanged, and with the exception of Natalie he was the greatest treasure in James' life.

"What did you do with him when you went away to war?" Lily asked curiously, tipping her head to the side as she studied Biscuit beneath long, snow covered lashes.

It was an innocent enough question. James could have answered it easily enough. He *should* have answered it easily enough, but when he opened his mouth to form the words they would not come. He was not ready to speak of the war, nor of anything that referenced it, no matter how small or inconsequential. "Who is Mr. Betram?" he asked instead, blatantly ignoring her question in favor of his own.

Instantly Lily's entire face seemed to crumple, and she turned her back on him to resume gazing out at the empty field. "Mr. Betram is my dog," she called over her shoulder. "He's a dear old thing, half blind and completely deaf, and I fear he got away from me." She spun around, her violet eyes wide and beseeching. "You have to help me find him, Captain Rigby. I fear he will freeze to death if I do not bring him home."

It was an accurate assumption. The winter elements were kind to neither human nor beast, and the snow was only going to increase in intensity with every hour that passed. Dark clouds warned of a storm blowing in from the east, a storm James believed would be the hardest hitting yet. It was one of the reasons he'd wanted to get his daily ride in so early in the morning; the other being he enjoyed the solitude. After being surrounded by noises for so long – gunfire, cannon blasts, the agonizing screams of men – James craved the silence.

For that reason and that reason alone he should have ridden on. He should have made an excuse, any excuse, and left Lily Kincaid to her own devices. She was the opposite of silence. The opposite of peace and calm and quiet. The rational part of his brain told him this, even as the other part – the bloody foolish part – had him nodding his head and following her footsteps, now almost completely covered in snow, down to the dilapidated fence line.

Biscuit followed, navigating the slippery terrain with ease, and stood obediently at his master's side, ears pricked towards the distant trees.

"Do you think he would return on his own?"

Lily shook her head. "No. Mr. Betram does not have a good sense of direction. He is probably wandering in circles. Oh, I have to find him. I absolutely must." She blinked, her lashes fluttering in rapid succession, and James was stunned to her eyes were sparkling with tears.

He knew women cried. He'd seen evidence of it in his own household, both from his mother and from his sister, but for some reason Lily did not strike him as a woman who shed tears easily, nor as one who used them for manipulation. She was too strong for that. Too honest. And yet here she was, fighting back tears over an old dog who had wandered into the woods.

It made him feel… protective. And the protectiveness made him wary. Wary of his feelings towards this slip of a sprite with her tangled mane of black silk and glimmering eyes made of jewels. Wary of what he might do because of them. Wary of what she would do in return.

He set his jaw, determined in that moment to turn on his heel and walk away, but then Lily sniffed — a tiny, unladylike sound of pure distress — and he was lost.

"I will find your Mr. Betram and return him to you." With practiced ease he slipped Biscuit's reins over the gelding's head and readied himself to mount, praying he wouldn't be made the fool when he attempted to use his right hand where he once would have used the left. "Where do you live?"

Lily pushed away from the fence and lifted her chin. "I am going with you, Captain Rigby."

James paused with his boot half in the stirrup and looked incredulously at her over his shoulder. "Into the woods? You bloody well are not. Go home, Lady Kincaid. The winds are picking up and heavier snow will soon be upon us. It is too cold for—"

"A woman?" she interrupted, lifting one dark brow.

"Please spare me your lecture on propriety, Captain Rigby. I brought Mr. Betram out here, and I will see him safely home. If your horse can carry two I will ride, if not I will walk, but be certain I will go with you either way."

James stared hard at her. She returned his stare unflinchingly, her posture as rigid as any general's. Hooking his fingers under the pommel of his saddle James mounted, swinging his right leg over without incident. He took the reins in hand, rubbing his thumb across the smooth leather. Biscuit tensed, his muscles rippling and shifting in anticipation of his master's cues. He mouthed the bit, clanking the metal between his teeth and tossing his head.

"Open the gate," James said at last.

"And?" Lily challenged.

"And you can ride with me."

CHAPTER SEVEN

FATE, LILY MUSED as she took in her new surroundings, was a complicated beast. Three hours ago she had been arguing with her mother and sister in the cozy confines of a parlor and now she was stranded with a man she barely knew in a small, forgotten caretaker's cottage tucked away in the middle of the forest.

Snow fell mercilessly outside the small, two room cottage, covering everything in a thick blanket of white. Standing on her tiptoes – the better to see beyond the drift that was rapidly accumulating outside the kitchen window – Lily peered up at the darkening sky, exposed in slivers of gray and angry blue through skeletal tree branches that clicked and clacked with the wind. A quiet whine had her reaching down to skim her hand across the top of Mr. Betram's head.

They'd found the wayward hound sitting in a thicket of brambles. He hadn't barked when they approached;

instead he simply wagged his tail and tilted his head, as though to say: *what took you so long?*

Unfortunately, by the time they retrieved Mr. Betram the winter storm had moved in with enough force to make a return trip nigh on impossible, and they'd been forced to seek shelter.

Lily had been the one to spot the cottage through the trees.

Sitting in the midst of an overgrown glen it was clearly abandoned, but the front door was unlocked and the furniture from the last inhabitants still in place. Besides a round wooden table with two mismatched chairs in the nook that served as the kitchen, there was a small writing desk, a musty smelling sofa, and a free standing bookcase stripped of books. Two wing chairs upholstered in faded blue fabric flanked a stone hearth and curtains, heavy with dust, framed the cottage's four windows. There was a bedroom as well, complete with a bed, which both Lily and James were resolutely ignoring although she'd caught his gaze straying towards the partially open door on more than one occasion.

Mr. Betram's fur was still damp from the snow and Lily wiped her palm on her skirt before she turned and directed her attention across the room to where James was kneeling in front of the stone hearth, attempting to start a fire.

His hand was cupped in front of his mouth and he was coaxing the flames to life with his breath, summoning them up from the depths of the kindling until they attacked the larger pieces of wood with a ferocity Lily found quite impressive.

"Have you done that many times before?" she asked, shuffling a few steps closer to the fire and extending her hands towards the warmth now emanating from the hearth. The flames crackled merrily, lighting the room in a soft glow. It was curiously cheerful, if she ignored the fact that she was stranded a good furlong from home with only a strange man for company. And yet, she did not feel ill at ease in James' presence. In truth he'd hardly said more than a dozen words to her since they began their journey, and she certainly did not feel in danger of being ravished. If anything he'd gone out of his way to avoid touching her, both on the horse and off, and Lily was left with the distinct impression that he was far more uncomfortable with the situation than she.

Her thought was proven correct when he leapt to his feet and jumped warily to the side, as though she were some carnivorous beast intent of devouring him whole instead of a tiny woman trying to get warm.

"Have you done that before?" she asked.

"Have I done what before?"

"Started a fire without a tinderbox."

For some reason, her clarification prompted a scowl. "Yes," he said shortly. "I have."

Captain James Rigby, she decided, was a man of few words. Which was perfectly fine, as she had more than enough for the both of them. "How long do you think we will have to stay here?"

Another innocent question, another scowl. He was standing to the side of the hearth, his countenance half in and half out of shadow. It made him appear forbidding. Ominous, even. Lily knew she should have been afraid. Any woman in her right mind would be. Instead she was… intrigued? Yes. *Intrigued* was as good a word as any to describe the fluttering sensation in her chest.

"When the snow stops and settles we can leave," he said.

Lily bit the inside of her cheek. "But it may not stop snowing for hours, and by then it will be dark."

James' expression was unreadable. "Then we will leave at first light."

At first light…

First light meant dawn. Dawn meant morning. Morning meant… She sucked in a breath. Morning meant spending the night here. With James. Alone.

For the first time, Lily considered her reputation and the possible repercussions that would follow if anyone found out where she'd been. She would be ruined, completely and irrevocably. Society was not kind to women who broke the unwritten rules; principle among them being one did *not* spend the evening alone with a gentleman without a proper chaperone. It hardly mattered if anything happened between her and Captain Rigby. She would be considered spoiled goods, and men seeking wives of high moral character did not want anything that was spoiled, no matter that they were hardly coming to the marriage bed a virgin themselves.

"Are you certain there is no way we can get home before nightfall?" Anxious now, she returned to the kitchen where her cloak was drying on one of the chairs. The fabric was still damp, but it was certainly wearable and all things considered she would much rather risk a chill than condemnation from her peers.

James remained by the hearth but his eyes followed her. When she turned with the cloak bundled tight in her arms he was staring at her unabashedly, an odd expression on his face. "I am sorry, but it does not seem likely. Biscuit will be unable to carry additional weight through the drifts and your dog—"

"I can carry him!" Lily cried. Except she couldn't, not really, and the look James gave her said as much. He cleared his throat.

"I will not... I will not do anything untoward, if that is why you are concerned."

"It's not," she muttered, looking away.

"You can sleep in the bedroom with the door closed, and I will be quite comfortable in front of the fire. I fear there is not any food, but hopefully we will be able to leave first thing in the morning and you will be home before breakfast."

Lily set her cloak aside and slumped into one of the kitchen chairs. It wobbled to the right, but held firm. Perching her elbow on the table, she adopted a scowl all her own. "And then what?" she challenged.

James' eyebrows darted together. "What do you mean?"

"Of course you do not understand. You are a *man*, and such things do not concern you." Her agitation increased, although whether it was at herself or him or the male species in general she could not be certain. *Stupid*, she chided herself. *You are so very stupid, Lily, and now you are going to have to pay the consequences for your impulsive actions. Unless...* She straightened in her chair. *Unless you really* do *become spoiled goods, and the man doing the spoiling is forced to offer marriage.*

She was grasping. She knew she was. Not to mention being quite underhanded, scheming, and devious – three traits she abhorred above all others. But with the deadline of Christmas breathing down her neck, what other choice did she have?

Family had always been of utmost importance to Lily. She would rather die than see her mother and sister be turned into beggars... Or, in this case, trick a man into marrying her by the worst means imaginable.

Her fingers began to thrum against the table. James would hate her in the end, and she would hate herself. But her mother and Elsa would have a future free from worry, and wasn't that all that mattered?

It really wasn't so different from what all the other women of her station did, she convinced herself as she watched James stoke the fire from beneath her lashes. Flocking to eligible men like pigeons to bread crumbs, pecking away until the poor fellow eventually gave up and gave in. She was simply being more upfront about the whole thing. In a not-quite-telling-the-truth sort of way.

If her plan failed she would be no better or worse off than before, the only exception being she really *would* be giving up her virginity, but then everyone would think she had anyways so really, what was the point of holding onto it?

With each day passing by quicker than the last it really was her best chance at securing a husband. Her *only* chance, if truth be told. Again she wondered at the nuances of fate. What intricate threads of destiny and happenstance had brought her to this very moment, with this very man? Would her choices this eve create ripples of consequence that ultimately destroy her future? Or was this somehow, someway, how things were supposed to happen? Her fingers increased in tempo, striking the table hard enough to send little jolts of pain shooting up into her wrist.

"Can you stop that incessant tapping?" Standing, James turned in a half circle and skewered her with a glare that would have no doubt brought a weaker female to tears. Lily merely lifted her chin and stared down her nose at him.

"They are my fingers," she said, "and I will do with

them what I please."

"Stubborn wench," he growled under his breath.

"Arrogant brute."

"Spoiled brat."

Lily sat up a little straighter. Two could play at this game. "Caper witted bounder."

"Featherbrained peagoose."

"Bacon-brained fatwit!"

James choked out a laugh. It sounded rusty, as though he hadn't laughed at anything in a very, very long time. "Bacon-brained fatwit?" he repeated, tilting his head to the side.

Lily shrugged. "It was the only thing I could think of."

"Are you not in the habit of slinging insults?"

"No," she said, biting back a smile. "Not precisely. I fear you bring out the worst in me." *In more ways than you can possibly imagine*, she added silently. Guilt weighed heavily on her shoulders, but she shoved it aside. She could not afford to feel guilty. Not if she wanted to do what needed to be done.

But how? Planning on losing her virginity was far different than actually doing the deed. Lily was accustomed to doing things herself, but she feared this was one of the few things she would be unable to accomplish solely on her own. She would need James' cooperation – his *willing* cooperation – if she wanted to set her plan in motion. Which meant she needed to stop insulting the man and start seducing him. Resolving herself to go through with the dirty deed, she did a quick glance around the room, taking stock of her surroundings.

Mr. Betram was curled up beneath the kitchen table, his soft rhythmic snores indicating he was sound asleep. Outside the small, cozy confines of the cottage snow continued to fall, banking up against the door and windows. There was no doubt about it. They would be stranded here for the remainder of the day and night… with no hope of leaving until morning.

"I am cold," she said abruptly.

Lifting up one of the heavy wing chairs, James positioned it until it sat directly in front of the hearth. "Sit," he said, gesturing with his arm before he stepped back. "I have to go find more firewood. There is not enough to get us through the night."

Lily froze halfway to the chair. "You are *leaving*?" she asked incredulously.

"I should not be gone long. I noticed a shed not far from here on our ride in. It most likely is part of the same estate this cottage belongs to, and may have wood inside it. I will not be gone long," he repeated, frowning at her expression. "You needn't be afraid."

"I am not *afraid*. I… Well, I…" But of course she couldn't give voice to the real reason she wanted James to stay – just imagining it forced a horrified chuckle past her lips. *Excuse me, but you cannot go anywhere because I need to seduce you. Why? Well, because I need you to take my virginity. Why? So you will feel obliged to marry me and my inheritance stays with my mother and sister instead of going to horrible Cousin Eustace. Oh, and by the by, all of this needs to be done before Christmas.* Pressing the back of her hand to her mouth, Lily sank into the wing chair and stared blindly into the fire. Another bubble of panicked laughter threatened, but she swallowed it down. Out of the corner of her eye she saw James hesitate at the door, twin lines of concern digging grooves into the corners of his chin.

"Go on," she said with a flippant wave of her hand. "Mr. Betram and I will be fine."

"Do not go outside," he said sternly.

Lily twisted in her chair to face him, digging her fingers into the dusty upholstery. "Outside?" she echoed. She forced a smile. "I fear only bacon-brained fatwits would dare go outside in this weather."

The walls of the cottage reverberated as James slammed the door behind him.

CHAPTER EIGHT

JAMES STRUCK OUT blindly into the snow, squinting into the wall of white and doing his best to forge a straight line. He kept an old decaying oak tree on his left. A short, fanned out mulberry on his right. Sucking in the cold, clear air by the mouthful he doubled over a short distance from the cottage, bracing his forearm across his knees and drawing a ragged breath.

There was no wood to gather. A box built into the wall next to the hearth housed more firewood than could be burned all winter. It had been an excuse. An excuse to get him out of the cottage. To get him away from *her* before he did something for which there was no excuse.

He couldn't breathe in her presence. Couldn't think. Couldn't move. She incapacitated him, sinking into his blood like the most deadliest of poisons, leaving him bewildered and off kilter, not knowing what way was up, what way was down.

The woman had made him *laugh*.

No one could do that, not even Natalie.

Running a hand through his hair – he had forgotten his hat inside – James pulled the curled ends taut with just enough pressure to cause pain. The pain cleared his head and helped him focus. He straightened, his resolve returning as he doubled back to check on Biscuit. The horse was tucked away in a three sided structure behind the cottage. He whickered contentedly as his master approached and James wrapped his arm around the gelding's neck, breathing in the familiar, calming scent of horse and hay.

"Are you going to be all right out here old chap?"

Biscuit, attentive as always, bobbed his head and swiveled his head to stare at James, his dark brown eyes both inquisitive and somehow amused, as though he knew his master's dilemma and thought it quite hilarious.

"Remember that gray mare you took a fancy to a few years ago?" James asked, speaking to Biscuit as though the horse could understand him, which James often thought he could. "Bellowed like a banshee every time she trotted past. You didn't have any shame, did you?"

Biscuit snorted.

"I did not understand you then, but I fear I do now."

He imagined how Lily would be as a horse. Beautiful, of course. An elegant thoroughbred with long legs, a lean body, and a refined head. High spirited, with a flash of temper. Stubborn, with a keen sense of intelligence. Difficult to ride, no doubt. Impossible to train. "Bloody hell," he muttered, rubbing a hand down his face.

He never should have stopped when he saw her on the road. Never should have dismounted. Never should have agreed to help find her damn dog. Now he would be forced to endure her presence not for a minute or an hour or even a day, but for an entire bloody *night*. A night in a cottage with walls so thin as to be nonexistent, listening to every toss and turn of her slender body as she slept. A night spent wondering what her creamy skin felt like… dreaming what her lips tasted like… imagining what—

With a curse James spun away from Biscuit and clipped the thought short. He needed to get himself under control, starting with exerting the same strict discipline over his emotions that he'd once used on the battlefield. Taking a deep, measuring breath he slapped a hand against his horse's broad shoulder in a gesture of farewell and started back towards the cottage, drawn by the soft glow of firelight emanating from the windows.

THE COLD RUSH of air woke her. It swept across her skin like ice, rousing her from a contented slumber filled with blurred images of church bells and white lace and a tall, rugged man with dark hair and piercing eyes.

Lily sat up with a start, wondering at the sudden pain in her neck until she realized she'd fallen asleep in the wing chair with her head tucked into the crook of her elbow. The fire had died low, the embers smoldering a deep red, indicating at least an hour of time had elapsed since she first closed her eyes. She heard the click of a door being closed, the quiet trod of footsteps, and then...

"I did not mean to wake you."

James' voice, low pitched and gravelly. The sound of it did the oddest things to her belly, making her feel as though she'd swallowed a dozen butterflies and the poor trapped creatures were flitting to and fro inside of her, frantically beating their wings in an effort to escape.

She remained in the chair but peered around the side of it, the better to see him. He stood silhouetted in the doorway, still as a statue. A fine layer of snow spread out across his broad shoulders. Flecks of white fell to the floor as he shrugged out of his heavy coat and set it aside on the window ledge. More snow glistened in his hair, melting to water as they studied each other, both unmoving.

"You do not have any wood," Lily noted.

James shook his head. "No," he said quietly.

"Why are you staring at me like that?" Suddenly self-conscious, she ran her fingers through her hair, knowing it must look a mess.

She'd tried a simple braid while James was outside, but her hair was still damp, the strands impossible to coerce into any semblance of order, and so she left them undone, letting the tangled curls dry by firelight. She dropped her chin, glancing down at her blue muslin gown. It was frightfully wrinkled, the fabric pulled taut in some placed and bunched in others. She bit the inside of her cheek and fought the urge to roll her eyes at herself. *Well done Lily*, she chided silently. *Certainly the best way to seduce a man is to have your hair a mess and your dress twisted up around your ankles*. Heavens. She wasn't very good at this, was she? Not that there was a book written on such things. Or, if there was, *she* had never read it.

"Stop it," she said as she lifted her head and realized James was still looking at her with the same forceful intensity, his eyes shimmering pools of dark in the soft glow of the room.

196

"Stop what?"

She gripped the armrest, frustrated that nothing was going as it should. "Stop *staring* at me as though… well, as though…"

"As though you are the most beautiful creature I have ever seen? I cannot," he said softly. "Not when your cheeks are flushed and your eyes are heavy with sleep and your lips are still wet from where you touched them with your tongue."

The butterflies went crazy. Lily went pale. *For a man who so rarely speaks*, she thought dazedly, *he certainly knows how to put the right words together*. And for once, for the first time she could ever remember, *she* was the one who couldn't think of a single thing to say. "I… I…"

Sliding out of his boots, James stepped forward. "I have tried to deny it, but you have felt it too, haven't you? In the ballroom, and then in the study." His expression bemused, as though he himself couldn't quite believe what he was saying, he shook his head. "You are without doubt the most antagonizing woman I have ever met… and the most desirable."

He was coming closer, Lily noted. Close enough for her to see his face without shadow. Close enough for her to touch. Close enough for him to reach out and gently, so gently as to barely be felt at all, cup her jaw and tilt her head up. His fingers threaded through the curls that framed her face and she leaned into his hand, helpless not to rub her cheek against the calloused skin of his palm. "T-thank you?" she managed to squeak, not certain if he was paying a compliment, not certain if she remembered what he'd said at all.

James growled low in his throat. It wasn't an angry sound. More of a frustrated surrender, although what he was surrendering she hadn't the faintest idea. "You should stop me," he said huskily. His mouth hovered a hair's breadth above her own, so close she could see the dark line of stubble on his chin. Their eyes met, their gazes held. For an instant Lily forgot to breathe, and when she finally released the air trapped in her lungs it came out in a rush.

"What if I do not want to?" she whispered.

Something flashed in James' eyes. Something dark. Something dangerous. Something so thrilling Lily felt her toes curl. "Then heaven help you," he murmured before he lowered his mouth to hers.

CHAPTER NINE

LILY WAS BURNING UP and it *wasn't* just because she was rolling around on the floor in front of the hearth, although that certainly had something to do with it. James was igniting flames inside of her... and he was setting her on fire.

Shadow and light reflected off his skin in equal measure as he settled himself beside her, resting, Lily could not help but notice, on the left side of his body. She laid flat on her back, one arm crooked behind her head, the other wound around James' waist as though it were the most natural thing in the world to mold her body against his.

He was kissing her slowly, his mouth moving with lingering softness over her lips, occasionally drifting lower to suckle the curve of her jaw or higher to tickle the sensitive bud of her earlobe.

In the past, Lily's kisses had always been stolen in the dark; a quick, almost painful mating of lip and tongue that left her mouth bruised and her heart feeling oddly hollow. Never in a hundred years had she imagined kissing could be like *this*.

James took his time with her, as though she were a fine wine meant to be sipped and cherished, not a rough shot of brandy to be quickly swallowed. His fingers were tracing an ever lengthening path down her body, starting from the flat plane of her stomach and moving down along the curve of her hip before reversing direction and gliding back up towards her breasts. Never truly touching where she ached for him most, and before long she was arching into his hand, silently begging for something she could not name but desperately wanted.

The kissing continued, filling her with an ache so keen she would have done anything to satisfy it. As though he could sense her growing frustration James murmured low in his throat, a soft, soothing sound that did little to alleviate her growing passion. She opened her eyes.

"Would you just hurry up with it?" she snapped before she quite knew what she was saying. Silence followed and she could feel her cheeks growing warmer. Now was *not* the time for talking, let alone barking orders. Oh, why couldn't she just be quiet and let what was going to happen bloody well happen? *Because you are an impatient hussy*, she scolded herself, *and you are going to ruin everything if you don't keep your trap shut. He is kissing you, is he not? Remain calm!* Easier to think than do, especially when it felt as though her entire body was being consumed by flames of desire. In hindsight she supposed it was a very good thing they had not kissed in the study, for instead of Sarah walking in on her sitting by herself in a dark room, she feared her friend would have interrupted something much more scandalous.

Why James was going through with it now when he had run before she did not have the faintest of ideas, nor was she about it question his reasons. All she knew was it felt heavenly, and despite the wrongness of it all it felt so *right*, and she really did want him to hurry.

As though he could sense the direction of her thoughts James paused in his kissing and nuzzled the curve of her neck. "I want to rip all the clothes off your body," he whispered against her warm skin, "and thrust inside of you so hard you scream my name."

"*Oh*," Lily breathed.

His smile was quick to reveal itself and even quicker

to retreat; a mere flashing of white teeth that never quite reached his eyes. "But that would be screwing, not lovemaking, and a woman like you is deserving of the latter."

Leaning towards him, she sat up on her elbow. The bodice of her dress brushed against his shirt and without thinking she reached out to toy with the starched edge of his collar. "A woman like me? And what sort of woman do you suppose I am?"

James did not hesitate in his response. "A woman who knows exactly what she wants."

If only he knew the half of it, Lily thought with the tiniest of grimaces. Again she succumbed to a deep, uncomfortable sense of guilt, but she pushed the feeling aside. She was doing what was best. After all, it wasn't as though she had twisted James' arm to get him down on the floor with her. He'd made that choice all on his own, and soon enough they both would pay the consequences.

"I do," she said. "I do know exactly what I want."

"And that is?"

She sat up straighter, reached behind her, and began to pluck at the stays on her dress. Her gaze steady on James, she allowed the tiniest, most catlike of smiles to curve her lips before she whispered, "You. I want you."

Her gown slithered down to her waist. James' eyes darkened with lust. He swallowed hard, his adams apple jerking in his throat. She felt an answering pull somewhere deep inside. A pull of need and desire she'd never felt before. Wordlessly he held out his arm. Lily fell into his embrace, and they both were lost.

LILY WAS A VIRGIN.

No, James corrected himself roughly, Lily *had* been a virgin.

Now, courtesy of him, she was not.

The evidence was there on one plump ivory thigh, a stain of crimson where there should have been only pale, flawless cream. The evidence had also been there during their lovemaking. A tightening of her mouth when he first pushed into her. A flicker of pain he had mistaken for pleasure. A cry he took for a moan. So many signs… and yet he'd still taken her on the floor like some rutting beast, deflowering her with all the finesse of a wild animal.

Disgusted with himself, James rolled away and sat up to face the fire as he fumbled with his clothes. The flames had all but sputtered out, casting the room in shadow and allowing a chill to creep into the air. He felt Lily stir behind him.

They dressed in silence. He found one of her stockings by the edge of the hearth and pushed it silently towards her. She pulled his shirt from beneath the winged chair and held it out, not meeting his gaze when he took it from her. It wasn't until James was attempting to button his shirt that he made a sound. It began as a low growl of frustration as he clumsily attempted to secure the buttons with one hand and ended with a snarl that was more befitting a wolf than a man.

"Let me," Lily said softly.

He turned from the fire to face her, rising up on his knees, still attempting to shove the buttons into place. "I do not need your help."

"Yes," she said, and this time she lifted her eyes to meet his, "you do."

Staring into those shimmering pools of amethyst James felt a deep sense of shame descend upon him. Shame that he could not do a thing so simple as button his own shirt. Shame that he had taken Lily's innocence. Shame that he was no longer the man he had once been. It filled him with anger, all that shame, and he reacted the only way he knew how: with deliberate cruelty.

"This is your entire bloody fault, you know."

Lily's eyes narrowed ever-so-slightly, but her voice remained calm. "It is my fault you cannot button your shirt?"

Another growl, this one more ferocious than the last. "If it were not for you and that damn dog I wouldn't even be here! And I wouldn't... I wouldn't..." But he could not form the words. He surged to his feet. Lily followed suit, albeit with an elegant grace he could not help but admire despite his anger. She'd donned her undergarments, but her dress must have been too difficult to put on by herself for it was still draped over the back of a chair. Her hair was loose and tangled, the dark curls spilling over her shoulders like a stream of black ink.

"Please leave Mr. Betram out of this. He did nothing wrong. Now if you would hold still, I can help you with your—"

"I DON'T NEED YOUR DAMN HELP!" He kicked out at a small end table, striking one of the slender legs. It cracked in half and the table, unsteady to begin with, crashed to the floor. Lily crossed her arms.

"Well I suppose that is one way to get firewood."

James spun away from her to brace his arm across the mantle of the hearth. His chest rose and fell with the force of his breaths, even as a flicker of confusion gave him pause. Why wasn't Lily running from him in horror? Any other woman he knew would have fled screaming by now, snow storm or no. He'd taken her virginity on the cold hard floor, blamed her for something that had been his own decision to make, and yelled at her with all the tact of a miserable old bear. Yet still she remained, composure in place, not a hint of hysteria in sight. "I wasn't always like this, you know," he said gruffly after a long, heavy pause.

"Moody and temperamental? I find that hard to believe."

"No." Frustrated, he turned and jerked his chin to the left. "Like *this*."

"You mean your missing arm? I assumed you lost it in the war, but I suppose you could have been born without it. Some people are, I hear." Lily shrugged, as though they were discussing something as benign as the weather instead of his crippling defect. "I am happy for you that you had it as long as you did, to be quite honest."

"Happy?" James said incredulously. "You are *happy*?"

"Yes. Imagine if you only ever had one arm. You never would have been able to experience life with two. Although perhaps that would have been better." The faintest of smiles lifted her mouth on one side. "I imagine you would have figured out how to button your own shirts by now."

Was she... *laughing* at him?

No, not laughing, James realized. Accepting. She was *accepting* him, one arm and all. The concept was so foreign – not to mention unexpected – that he quite simply could not think of anything to say.

"I fear I am quite tired," Lily said, interrupting the silence before it could stretch into something bordering on the uncomfortable. "Would you mind stoking the fire while I ready for bed?" Without waiting for a response she headed for the bedroom, only to hesitate with her fingers curled around the knob. "You *will* sleep with me, won't you? For body warmth," she said quickly before he could manage a word. "I would hate to catch a chill. Come along, Mr. Betram."

With a groan and a mumble the old beagle surged to his feet and waddled after his mistress, leaving James staring after both of them in slack jawed astonishment.

CHAPTER TEN

28 days until Christmas
The Winswood Estate

"SARAH, I NEED to speak with you at once." It was only half past ten in the morning when Lily marched into her friend's foyer and handed her cloak and hat to a servant, but she did not think for one moment that Sarah was still abed. Thanking the maid who had taken her outer garments, she proceeded down the front hallway and into the music room without invitation.

As predicted (from many other early morning visits just like this one) she found Sarah sitting behind the pianoforte, her fingers hovering in tense anticipation above the ivory keys and her face scrunched tight in concentration.

"I cannot play this one sequence of notes," she complained without looking up. "The bridge is particularly difficult, but Devlin talked me into doing a recital before Christmas Eve dinner and I have to do it perfectly."

"Where is that husband of yours?" Lily asked before she collapsed into a chair and propped her feet up on a cushioned footrest. The room was warm courtesy of a crackling fire, and she rolled up the sleeves of her light yellow morning dress to mid forearm. The other fireplaces in the sprawling manor must have been going as well, for on her way up the long, twisting drive she'd noted smoke spiraling from all four chimneys, the plumes of gray standing out in sharp contrast against the clear blue sky.

It was a lovely day, last night's raging storm only evident in the thick blanket of freshly fallen snow. If she tried hard enough Lily could almost imagine yesterday had never happened at all, until she moved a certain way and the soreness between her thighs said otherwise.

She and James had woken at first light and left the cottage as dawn was cresting on the horizon. He brought her back to where he found her and they parted ways without a word.

No promises spoken. No betrothals made. Just one long, lingering look that instantly heated her cheeks and caused the breath to stutter in her lungs. When Lily returned home – sneaking through the servant's door around the side – everyone had still been abed with the exception of the cook, who had taken one look at Lily's disheveled appearance, rolled her eyes, and slipped silently back into the kitchen.

She'd bathed her face and chest in cold water, exchanged one set of clothes for another, and set off at once for the Winswood estate which was only a brisk walk down the lane in the opposite direction of where she'd gone the day before.

If Sarah thought it was odd of her friend to show up before breakfast without a carriage or even a horse, she made no mention. Then again, Lily's eccentricities were well known, especially to Sarah. Adjusting the skirt of her rose colored morning dress, the blond played a few more notes before she turned the sheet music over with a huff and stood up. "Devlin is in London on business. He left directly after the ball, and should be home by the end of the week. Do you want tea and scones? I believe Cook just made fresh ones."

"That would be lovely."

Sarah waited for the refreshments to be brought out on a silver platter before she sat down across from Lily. She raised her eyebrows. "Well?" she said expectantly. "What is it you have to tell me?"

Selecting a scone, Lily bit into warm dough, not realizing she was half starved until she wolfed down the first scone and started on the second. "Why do you assume I have something to tell?"

"Your mother came looking for you yesterday afternoon. I told her you were upstairs changing, and that we were going into town for a bit of shopping."

Relief washed over Lily like a wave, only to be followed by something distinctly less comfortable. If her mother believed she had spent the day and night with Sarah, then her reputation would not be ruined as she feared... except her virginity truly had been lost. The irony of it caused her to laugh, and Sarah's expression grew tight with concern.

"Lily, what is it? I can tell something is bothering you. I did not want to say anything at the ball, but you have been acting very odd as of late. Is this because of your father?"

Yes, it *was* because of her father, but not in the way Sarah meant. Lily took a deep breath. She needed to tell Sarah everything, if only so someone else could share her burden. It was a selfish thing to do, but then hadn't she already proven that she was, in fact, quite selfish? Taking a sip of tea to settle her stomach, she told her friend everything in a rush, beginning with Mr. Guthridge's visit and ending with that very morning when she and James parted ways without a word spoken between them.

Sarah's eyes grew wider and wider with every revelation, but she did not interrupt and Lily was grateful for her silence. When she was finished, when there was no detail left unsaid, she slumped back in her chair, threw an arm up over her face, and groaned loudly. "And so you see I am now quite ruined. James will not have me, Christmas is right around the corner, and we will soon lose everything to Cousin Eustace." She opened one eye and peeked under her wrist. "Have I left anything out?"

"Heavens," Sarah said dazedly, "I hope not."

Lily's smile was both wry and self-deprecating. "I do not know what to do," she admitted. "I thought sleeping with James would solve all of my problems, but now I fear I have only made them worse. What if he tells someone what we did? No man would have me after that."

"I do not know Captain Rigby overly well, but from what I have heard of him he seems like a man of high moral character." Sarah's smile was encouraging. "So you should not worry about him spreading idle gossip."

"Yes, no one need know I've lost my virginity until

my future husband discovers my lack of innocence on our wedding night and tosses me out on my ear."

"I wouldn't worry about that either. Seeing as your cousin will soon have all of your money and you will not be in possession of a dowry, no man of consequence is likely to look twice at you."

Lily dropped her arm to stare incredulously at her friend. "Is that supposed to make me feel better?"

"No, I suppose not." Sarah took a thoughtful bite of her scone. "But I am confident we will come up with a solution. After all, what happened to you is not so different than what happened to me, and look how well everything turned out with Devlin and I!"

"I fear James is not the sort of man to profess his love over a sleigh ride through the park. He did not say a word, Sarah. Not a *word* when we parted ways." The anxiety of it all settled in her chest like a stone, weighing her down and leaving her rooted in the chair where she once would have paced circles around the room. What was she going to *do*? For once, Lily did not have an answer.

"Well, did *you* say anything when you parted ways this morning?" Sarah asked.

"I… No," she said after she thought about it. "I

didn't."

"There you have it, then!" Sarah said excitedly. A bit *too* excitedly, Lily thought with a scowl, given the dower circumstances. "*You* did not say anything so *he* did not say anything. Perhaps he is sitting in a drawing room somewhere at this very moment, having the same exact conversation we are!"

"I highly doubt that."

"Oh, posh." Sarah waved her hand in the air. "What do you know? Look at what a muck of things you've made so far. I must say, this is not at all your best scheming. Which makes it all the more interesting, does it not?"

"You are talking in riddles," Lily said irritably, "and not being at all helpful."

"I am being incredibly helpful," Sarah corrected with a beaming smile. "And I have come up with a perfect solution."

Hope flickered inside Lily's heart, hesitant as a newly born flame. *Was* there a way to fix everything? Sarah certainly seemed to think so. She bit the inside of her cheek, telling herself not to get too excited even as the anticipation nearly drove her up and out of her chair. She wrapped her arms around her chest to contain the pounding of her heart and leaned forward. "Which is?"

"It is quite simple, really. All you have to do is ask Captain Rigby to marry you."

JAMES HAD NOT moved from his chair for the past hour. He sat in silence, staring down at his desk and the blank piece of blank parchment resting on top of it. The words that needed to be written on the parchment – a simple letter to a solicitor – echoed in his mind, but try as he might he could not summon the concentration necessary to commit them to paper. His mind was preoccupied, his thoughts very much elsewhere.

As the second hour began to pass his muscles grew stiff but still he remained in the chair. Not moving, just staring, as though the empty page before him would reveal all the answers he sought if he but studied it long enough.

"I knocked, but you did not answer. What are you doing?"

James jumped at the sound of his sister's voice. He'd been so deep in thought he hadn't heard her at the door nor, it seemed, noticed when she entered the room. Dressed in a drab gray dress with a white shawl wrapped around her shoulders she looked old beyond her years… and far more serious than any sixteen year old girl should ever appear. "I was thinking about something," he said honestly. "What are you doing awake and dressed?" He glanced out the window, thinking perhaps more time had passed than he initially believed, but the sun was still rising in the sky, indicating the hour to be quite early.

Natalie shrugged her shoulders beneath the shawl. "I could not sleep." Tucking her legs up, she settled into a chair, but kept her gaze on him, her blue eyes inquisitive. "You did not come home last night."

"No." He did not offer an explanation, for what could he say? *I did not come home because I was in the process of ruining a young woman's life. What woman? Oh, the very same one you met at the Heathcliff's ball.* He hoped Natalie would be satisfied with the fact that he was home *now* and leave the matter alone, but he should have known better. His sister had always been curious and, when it came down to it, often quite nosy. As a girl she'd been caught eavesdropping behind doors on more than one occasion, a habit which seemed unbroken even after all this time.

"Did you go into town?" she asked, resting her chin on her knees and looking very much like the baby sister he had left instead of the waif like, sad eyed woman he'd returned home to. "Or to the pub? Or perhaps you went—

216

"Leave it alone Natty," he said, a hard edge to his voice. Her face paled, and he could have kicked himself. "What I meant to say, is my absence is nothing you should concern yourself with... sweetheart." The endearment sounded odd even to his own ears, but he was determined to be softer with his sister, and what better way than to begin using terms of affection? Unfortunately, it did not have the effect on Natalie he would have hoped.

"Do *not* call me that," she said fiercely.

James' forehead creased in bewilderment. "Sweetheart, I did not mean—"

"STOP IT! STOP IT! STOP IT!" she shrieked, and in the aftermath of her sudden outburst they were both silent. Natalie was breathing heavily, her small chest pushing in and out quick as a bird's.

James noted her fingers were pressed into the arms of the leather chair so hard her knuckles shone white in the drowsy light of morning. She was terrified, he realized dumbly. Absolutely terrified. But of what? Of him? Somehow, he did not think he was the cause. The shell shocked expression on her face was the same he'd seen worn by men on the battlefield after they'd witnessed an unspeakable horror. "Natty," he began, careful to keep his voice calm so as not to upset her further, "is there something you are not telling me?"

She shook her head quickly. Too quickly, James thought.

"Did… did something happen to you while I was away?" he persisted, not willing to let the matter drop until he had answers. They could not go on like this. *He* could not go on like this: walking on eggshells around his own sister, afraid of what to say, never knowing what to do. It was time she faced her demons and started healing. It was time they *both* faced their demons and started healing. For some reason, at that very moment, Lily's face rose unbidden in his mind. He saw her quick smile. Her violet eyes, filled with laughter. Her long, silky legs, wrapped around his hips…

"I do not wish to speak of it," his sister whispered, efficiently drawing him back to the present.

"Natty…"

"You should marry," she said suddenly.

James blinked, as caught off the guard by the sudden change in conversation as he was by the topic. "I should… I should what?"

"Marry," she repeated. "I think it would be good for

you to have someone."

"I have you," he said automatically, but Natalie only shook her head, her smile impossibly sad.

"You need someone else," she insisted. "Someone to help care for you and this house. Someone to make you laugh."

Lily makes me laugh.

"You deserve to be happy again." Natalie's blue eyes were wide and beseeching. James looked away, unable to meet her gaze and the truth he saw reflected within. Pain recognized pain, he thought. Which was why his sister could so clearly see what he kept hidden inside.

"I have not thought of marriage." A lie. It was *all* he'd been thinking about since he woke up that morning tangled in the arms of a beautiful, mischievous sprite. He knew what he had to do. What he was honor bound to do. He had taken Lily's virginity, something that should have exclusively belonged to her future husband, and while she had been a willing party, he would not let her face the consequences of their actions alone.

And yet James could not help but think it would not be such a consequence. He knew nothing about Lily Kincaid except the husky sound of her laughter, the stubborn glint that gleamed in her eye when she'd set her mind to something, and her willingness to risk her life for an old hound anyone else would have abandoned to the wilderness. More lies. He also knew the taste of her skin. The tempo of her heart. The sound of her moan… He shook his head to clear it, and dared a quick glance at Natalie. His sister was studying him intently, the oddest of smiles on her pale face.

"Do you know what I would like for Christmas above all else?" she asked.

James did not have the faintest of ideas. "A new dress?" he ventured.

Natalie shook her head. "A sister. I should very, *very* much like a sister." Leaving him gaping after her, she gathered her skirts and skipped from the room.

CHAPTER ELEVEN

25 days until Christmas

TIME WAS RUNNING OUT.

Lily knew it. Her mother knew it. Elsa knew it. Even Mr. Betram knew it, if his constant nightly howling was any indication.

From James she'd heard not a word, which only made everything all the worse for she thought of him constantly. He invaded her dreams every night without fail, sliding into her subconscious as stealthily as a shadow and filling her mind with the sound of his husky voice, the serious slant of his mouth, the touch of his skin…

During the day it was not much better. Even though only three days had passed since their time together in the cottage she must have imagined him a hundred, nay, a *thousand* times. If she did not keep herself busy she thought of him. If she slept she thought of him. It seemed with every breath she drew she thought of him, until she was so consumed it was nearly impossible to think of anything else. Which was why, on a bright, sun drenched afternoon, she found herself with Sarah at the very last place she desired to be: a holiday fair in the middle of town.

Shop owners hawked their wares from every street corner. A man with a white beard pushed a wooden cart filled to the brim with wreaths. Children ran through the crowd selling bright red ribbons. A group of women, wearing matching green cloaks and fur muffs, sang cheerful carols at the top of their lungs.

Sarah, boasting a bright smile, held fast to Lily's arm and steered them both towards a vendor selling steaming hot cups of chocolate. There was a rather long line – no surprise given the frigid temperature – and Sarah turned to Lily after they'd shuffled their way into it. "Isn't this positively delightful?" she asked, raising her voice to be heard above the din.

Lily did a quick, sweeping glance of the organized chaos and struggled not to grimace. "Yes," she lied. "Delightful."

Sarah's face fell. "You are not having a good time at all, are you?"

The line moved forward a few feet, and they moved with it. Lily sighed. "I am trying. Truly I am. But all of the festivities—"

"—are only reminding you that Christmas is right around the corner," Sarah finished. "I should have taken that under consideration. We can leave, if you would like."

"No." Lily shook her head from side to side, causing the hood of her cloak to fall back. She'd pinned her hair up in a circular braid that wound around the crown of her head and woven red ribbon through the thick, glossy strands in an attempt to be festive. Unfortunately, it seemed not even pretty ribbon could boost her spirits, but she was not about to let her problems affect Sarah's happiness. "We will get hot chocolate and walk all around. I saw a booth selling glass snowflakes when we first came in. I should like to buy one for Elsa, and find something for Mother as well."

Sarah's expression was doubtful. "Are you certain?"

"Yes, I—I…" She trailed off in sudden alarm.

"Lily? What is it? What's wrong?"

But Lily wasn't listening. She was, instead, doing her best to hide behind Sarah, but the blond kept spinning in a circle, making it quite difficult. "Stop moving!" she hissed, peeping up and over her friend's shoulder at the man she'd spotted across the square. Even from this distance there was no mistaking James' tall, rugged frame for anyone else's.

"What on earth..." Sarah breathed, before she followed Lily's gaze and picked James out from the crowd as well. It wasn't very difficult to do. Even if he wasn't dressed in all black he still would have stood out from the rest of the merry goers, as different from them as the moon was from the sun. He stood by himself off to the side, his expression shuttered. "Is that him? Is that Captain Rigby?"

Lily nodded.

Sarah squealed.

"Oh, this is perfect! You must go over and speak with him. And for heaven's sake, get out from behind me." Sarah's frown was disapproving. "I have never seen you act like this in all my life. Why are you hiding?"

"I am not hiding," Lily said automatically. Except she was. Feeling rather sheepish, she straightened up and stepped to the side of her friend, never taking her eyes from James. He looked well, she decided. In an I-am-angry-at-the-entire-world sort of way, which was so very typical she could not help but smile. Her smile was quick to fade, however, as she wondered if he'd been thinking of her as she'd been thinking of him.

Did he lay awake at night remembering their time spent together? Or was she already forgotten, a fleeting star in an endless sky of flickering lights? Suddenly, Lily didn't know if she possessed the courage to find out.

"We need to leave," she hissed, ducking back down behind Sarah's shoulder.

"Too late," Sarah said, sounding far too cheerful given the circumstances. Then, in a louder voice she said, "Captain Rigby, is it not? We were introduced, albeit briefly, at my home. And this" – reaching behind her, she grabbed a hold of Lily's arm and forcibly dragged her forward – "is my dearest friend Lady Lily Kincaid."

"We have met," James said curtly. His eyes were cold, his countenance inscrutable. Lily could feel the words she wanted to say withering up and dying inside of her throat. For someone who always had an answer for everything, it was a foreign – not to mention unpleasant – sensation.

"Well then," Sarah said slowly as her gaze traveled from Lily to James and back again. "If you have already met, no doubt you wish to have a moment alone to be reacquainted. I will be right over there if you need me." And she was gone, and even though they were surrounded by people in the middle of a very public town square, Lily had never felt more alone in all her life.

Say something, she thought desperately. *Anything, say anything!* "Mr. Betram is doing well," she blurted.

"I am glad to hear it."

Lily waited for him to say something else, but it seemed that was it. *I am glad to hear it.* Five short words which had nothing to do with the matter at hand. Inexplicably she was filled with an irrational surge of anger, most of it directed at the man standing in front of her. After all, *he* had been the one to approach *her*. And all he had to say for himself, after two days of silence, was 'I am glad to hear it'? Her nostrils flared. "Could I speak with you," she gritted out, "in a more private setting?"

James inclined his head and began to move through the crowd, his strides so long she had to pick up the hem of her skirts and run to catch up.

By the time they'd rounded the corner of the fabric store and stopped short in a narrow alley framed by two sizable brick buildings Lily was out of breath and in the grips of a temper she hadn't felt in quite some time. "You," she wheezed, jabbing her pointer finger at James, "are a pompous jackass."

His eyebrows lifted. "Are we back to this?" He shifted his weight and leaned against one of the buildings. Flickers of sunlight, beaming in through the front of the alley, played across his face, illuminating the scruff of beard he'd failed to shave and a tiny white scar on the corner of his chin she hadn't noticed until now. "Do you always toss insults about when you don't know what else to say?"

Lily crossed her arms tight over her chest and glared. "I have *plenty* to say."

"Well then, go on."

Her mouth opened. Closed. She thought of the nights she'd spent awake staring at the ceiling and rehearsing, word for word, what she would tell James if given the opportunity. Now her chance was here, and she couldn't think of a single thing to say.

So she said everything.

Beginning with the death of her father and ending with the cottage she left nothing out, and when she was finished it felt as though a great weight had been lifted from her shoulders. The guilt was gone, and even though her confession meant James would never marry her and everything was ruined, she was content with the knowledge she had not tricked him into a marriage they would both come to regret.

Having been unable to look him in the eye while she was spewing out the truth in quick, hot bursts of half sentences and jumbled words, she lifted her chin to gauge his reaction... and felt her jaw drop when she saw he was smiling. "Do you... Do you not understand what I have told you?"

"Oh, I understand perfectly," he said.

"And you are not angry?" she ventured hesitantly.

He pushed away from the wall and stepped forward, crowding her back against the brick. It felt warm against her exposed neck, but the warmth of the sun drenched wall was nothing compared to heat rapidly pooling in her belly.

"Furious," he whispered. Their eyes met and held a second before he tilted his head to the side and claimed her mouth with his.

The kiss was long and lingering and so brutally passionate it left Lily gasping for breath even after James stepped back. He stood in the middle of the alley, his shadow flung up over her left shoulder. His expression was impossible to read, his body taut.

"What... what was that for?" she gasped.

"A test," he said.

She fought the urge to grind her teeth. Getting the man to say more than three words was the equivalent of prying a rusty nail from a hard knot of wood. "What *kind* of test?"

"One to see if what we had before was real or feigned."

Oh. "And?"

"I believe it was real." He rubbed the side of his face where her fingers had pressed while they kissed. "Why tell me everything now? You could have gotten away with it, and I would never have been the wiser."

Lily shook her head. "I do not want you to want me because you feel obligated or… or honor bound."

"And if I wanted you for you?"

She regarded him sadly. Perhaps, in another time, in another place, they could have been perfect for each other. She liked to think what she felt for him was not born of desperation, but how could she ever know for certain? Despite having shared their bodies they were still strangers. They'd really only met twice, at the ball and then on the road that ultimately led to the cottage. "How could you? I just admitted that I wanted to trick you into marrying me." The shame of it brought a rush of color to her cheeks. "You deserve someone far better than I. You are a good man, James Rigby." She ached to touch him, and burrowed her hands deep into the pockets of her cloak, her hands curling into fists so tight it caused her nails to bite into her palms. "An honorable man. Even a kind one, beneath all your gruffness." She managed a smile. "You need a woman who is quiet and soft and gentle. I am none of those things, nor do I fear will I ever be.

Something flickered across James' face. Surprise? Anger? Regret? Lily could not be certain. She began to say goodbye, but the words remained locked inside her throat. Realizing she was perilously close to tears she let her body say what her voice could not.

The embrace was painfully quick. Her arms, wrapped around his neck. Her lips, pressed against his cheek. Inhaling the scent of him. Memorizing the feel of him. One last, longing stare.

And then she ran.

YOU DESERVE SOMEONE *far better than I.*

Lily's voice played back in James' mind as he watched her hurry away. He kept his gaze trained on her dark blue cloak for as long as he could, but when she went behind a vendor's cart he lost her to the crowd.

The bloody woman thought she wasn't good enough for him.

Clearly, she was a bit mad.

Yet still he wanted her in a way he'd never wanted anything in his entire life. It consumed him, this want, until he could not think of anything else. The taste of her lingered on his lips and he stared at the place where she'd been far longer than he should have.

When the sounds of the holiday fair finally began to wind down and the sun was heavy in the sky James returned home. The house was empty – Natalie was staying the night at a friend's – and, for the first time in a very long time, he yearned for sound. He needed light and laughter to fill the carnivorous hole inside of him, a hole forged by death and decay and dark things no man should ever bear witness. He needed someone loud and boisterous. Someone who wasn't afraid to tell him when he was being an ass or, he thought with a smile, a bacon-brained fatwit.

He wanted to hear the house ring with the sounds of children laughing, James realized as he sat heavily behind his desk. And he wanted Natalie to have a woman she could speak to. Someone strong she could admire and trust. Someone to help her face the demons that haunted her.

His fingers began to drum on the hard wood of the desk. If given the choice, he would have preferred to take his time. To court Lily as she deserved to be courted. To woo her and love her and whisper sweet nothings in her air as they danced in the moonlight. But he wasn't that man anymore, and she didn't have the patience to be that woman.

Would it work? Christmas was little more than three weeks away. He knew the strain of it must have been hanging over Lily's head like a guillotine, and he did not begrudge her her actions, nor condemn her for them. She'd been willing to risk all for her family, but even with the solution to all of her problems right in front of her she had not gone through with it. There must have been a reason above and beyond her moral conscience. He liked to think that reason was him, but he could not know until he did what needed to be done.

Resting his elbow on the table, James buried his face in the hard, leather skin of his palm and for the first time since his return, murmured a prayer.

CHAPTER TWELVE

Christmas Eve

EIGHT HOURS. That was all that stood between her and complete financial ruin. Standing to back of a caroling group, hidden in shadow and half-heartedly mouthing along the words to a song she knew by heart, Lily could not help but think of her many failures.

If she'd only listened to her father more and argued with her mother less. Paid attention during her tutoring sessions. Learned how to sew a decent stitch. Feigned interest in a man when he was talking to her, even if he was terribly boring. Played the pianoforte with grace. Bitten her tongue instead of blurting out the first thought that entered her head. So many little things she'd been too stubborn to fix and now here she was without a prayer of finding a husband.

And still, even after everything, she thought of James.

It had been twenty four long, lonely days since the holiday fair. Twenty four mornings of waking up and racing downstairs to see if any note had been delivered during the night. Twenty four afternoons spent at home on the offhand chance he happened by to see her. Twenty four nights spent dreaming of him.

She was absolutely miserable, and she knew her misery was born of a broken heart. The stupid man had made her fall in love with him and then she'd mucked it all up. At first she tried to convince herself it was simply a passing fancy. After all, he was her first. But she knew, deep in her soul, that no matter if one man or a hundred came after him, he would always be her only.

The only one to make her laugh.

The only one to make her yearn.

The only one to touch her heart.

This is what happens when you fall in love with broken men, she thought darkly. *You end up being the one broken in the end.*

The carolers, immersed in their songs and feelings of goodwill, moved onwards down the lane towards the next house, lighting the way with candles and torches decorated with ribbons and holly. Lily stayed in the shadows, letting her mother and Elsa go on without her. She was not fit for company, and she did not want her mood to ruin the night for anyone else.

"I thought the point of caroling was to sing," a deep, achingly familiar voice drawled from the shadows.

Lily jumped and whirled, kicking out a spray of snow. She squinted into the darkness, trying to decipher shape from shadow, and could not help but gasp aloud when James stepped forward from beneath the eaves of a shed. He held a single candle, the light from it illuminating his face.

"What… what are you *doing* here?"

He stepped closer and the circle of light enveloped her in its rosy glow. "I asked Lady Heathcliff where I could find you. She was very helpful."

Sarah, who had begged off the evening's festivities because of a head cold. Sarah, who had known James would come looking for her. Sarah, who was not long for this world once Lily got her hands on her.

She shook her head. "I do not understand."

"I know," James said softly. "It should not make sense, but it does."

"*What* does?"

235

He held her gaze, his dark, soulful eyes unblinking and for once she could read the emotion swirling behind the wall of stone. It struck a chord in her heart, pulling her towards him even as she dug in her heels and did her best to resist. "You. Me. Us. *We* make sense," he said. "I do not know how, or why, but we bloody well do. You know it as well. I know you do."

Lily bit her lip and looked away. In the distance she could hear the joyful notes of a familiar Christmas ballad and she was reminded of the date, and all the implications it carried with it. She twisted away, giving him her shoulder. "You are only saying this because you feel obligated. You shouldn't," she said, more sharply than she intended. "There will be no... no complications from our time spent together and it was as much my fault as it was yours, so do not think you have ruined me. I ruined myself."

"Lily."

She tensed at the sound of her name on his lips. Had he ever spoken it aloud before? She didn't know. She could not remember. "If you are here out of pity or some foolish sense of—"

He stepped forward, closing the distance between them in one long, loping stride. His hand fell heavily on her arm and he spun her around. Yanked her tight against his chest. "I came here for *you*," he said fiercely.

She tilted her head back, searching for the truth in his eyes. What she saw left her breathless. Still, she dared not believe what was right in front of her. Dared not believe such a thing was even possible. "If that is true, where have you been?"

"In Edinburgh and London and every other bloody place I could think of to secure a special marriage license."

At that, Lily's vocal chords quite simply stopped working. Her lips parted, but no sound came out save a squeak that James seemed to find quite amusing if his sudden grin was any indication. It was there and gone again before she had time to blink, but the trace of it lingered in his eyes and touched something deep inside her heart.

"I've been granted one from the archbishop," he said, answering her unspoken question, "and the parish priest is ready to marry us. We can be wed tonight, if you wish it, and you need never worry again for the future of your family. Between myself and your father's will, they shall be well provided for."

"T-tonight?" Lily croaked. "But... but it is all

happening so quickly."

James steadied her against his chest when she would have pulled back. His arm tightened around the curve of her hip, holding her against him, refusing to let go. "Do you think my feelings will be any less a month from now? Or a year? For the first time in a long time I know exactly what I want, Lily Kincaid. And nothing will change that."

"You barely know me." Lily didn't know why she was resisting. This was what she wanted. What she'd dreamed of. But to wish for something wondrous to happen and then to actually be granted such a wish were two very different things entirely. How could James possibly want her? She'd been rude to him. Tricked him. Called him names. *And loved him,* a softer voice intruded. *Listened to him. Held him while he slept. Treated him as a man, not a monster. Seen him as he is now, not who he used to be.*

James slowly slid his arm from around her back. He cupped her jaw, his thumb reaching up to trace along the delicate curve of her cheekbone. "I know you are intelligent. I know you are witty. I know you are beautiful. I know you are brave and strong and stubborn to a fault. I know you make me want to be a better man." He took a deep breath. "I am not healed, Lily. I have scars on the outside and within. I am not perfect, but I know we are perfect for each other. We may have only known each other for a short time, but my soul knows you, Lily. I *know* you."

Her lips parted. She scrambled to think of the right thing to say but her heart was melting, and her mind was quickly following suit. In the end, she said what she felt in the depths of her soul. Staring up into James' eyes, seeing the love shining through as bright as the stars in the sky, she whispered, "I know you."

And she did.

EPILOGUE

IN THE END, they were not married on Christmas Eve.

Lily did not want James to think the only reason she was marrying him was to preserve the inheritance, and even though he was adamant to the contrary, she stood firm.

"Stubborn brat," he told her with great affection.

"Goose livered nincompoop," she replied before she looped her arms around his neck and kissed him senseless.

They told Lily's mother on Christmas morning. She wept, and declared it was the best present she had ever received. The two families dined together, and Natalie and Elsa were already on their way to becoming the very closest of friends.

The only damper on an otherwise perfect evening was the arrival of Cousin Eustace and Venetia, who came uninvited while dessert was being served. Lily still wasn't certain what James said to her cousin; all she knew was Eustace vowed not to lay a finger on her dowry and left with all haste, dragging his squabbling wife behind him.

They were married the day after Christmas. True to his word James had been able to procure a special license and the parish priest, a short, bald man with twinkling blue eyes and a ready smile, wed them before their closest family and loved ones.

When Lily and James emerged from the church shoes were thrown – for luck – and as if on cue snow began to fall from the sky. Tipping her head back, Lily caught a flake on her tongue. With her face tilted up towards the heavens she saw, for an instant, a bright flash of light. Warmth spread over her, and she tightened her grip on her husband's arm. He gazed down at her, and she knew the love in his eyes was echoed in her own.

Lily still wasn't sure exactly when it happened, or how. She only knew she loved the man standing beside her with all her heart, and she was blessed to be able to spend the rest of her life with him. To keep a home with him. To raise a family with him. To love him unconditionally, until her last breath was taken.

Their future together would not be an easy one, Lily knew that as well. They would argue and fight – they were both too stubborn not to. But through all the trials and tribulations she knew their love would shine like a beacon, brightening their lives and always bringing them back to each other in the end.

Again she looked to the sky, this time with understanding. "Thank you Father," she whispered, "and Merry Christmas."

ABOUT THE AUTHOR

Jillian Eaton grew up in Maine and now resides in Pennsylvania. When she isn't writing, Jillian is doing her best to keep up with her three very mischievous dogs. She loves horses, coffee, getting email from readers, ducks, and staying up late finishing a good book.

She isn't very fond of doing laundry.

www.jillianeaton.com

Printed in Great Britain
by Amazon